The Way of the Exiled

by

Natasja Rose

ISBN: 9781535105507

Characters in this story are completely fictional. Any
resemblance to real places, events, names or people is
entirely coincidental, and no direct association
should be inferred.

3

Table of Contents

Prologue

"The sands of the desert are ever-shifting, but the wise man watches them, rather than be caught unaware by the storm."

-Ancient Noorinian Proverb

The desert sun beat down harshly on the ragged group, staggering onward through the endless sands, fear and death biting at their heels.

Overhead, birds circled, and the boy clutched the precious bundle in his arms tighter. Tears stung his eyes, but he refused to let them fall; he didn't have the water to waste. Angry determination forced him forward another step. He couldn't fail now!

The oasis-city they had fled was far behind them, lost to sight, but the boy thought that he could still hear the clash of steel, the sickening thump of bodies hitting the ground. The image of his father, standing over the cooling form of his older brother, yelling for him to take the other children and run, as he matched blades with the Warlord who thought to take what was never his to claim, was burned into his mind's eye. So had been the boy's last sight of his home, with the tall, indominable man who had loved and raised him crumpled in a heap at the gates, his blood staining the thirsty sand.

Curse the thrice-damned Lord Mal to the lowest circle of the Afterlife's torments! May he suffer as his countless victims had, and if the Gods didn't feel like setting the Warlord to rights, Owain would happily do it for them! One day, when he was stronger, strong enough to rescue what remained of his people and take back their home.

At the back of the group, someone stumbled and fell. The youth turned back, watching as another boy helped the younger child to their feet. He scanned the rolling dunes that surrounded them; there was little shelter to be had, but they needed to rest. To go on would be to push the youngest beyond their already strained endurance.

There! A small rock formation, with shadows that indicated caves or hollows at its base. Better than nothing. The boy led his fellow survivors to the rocks, looking up in alarm as a larger shadow fell across them. They broke into a desperate, staggering run as the shadow grew, swooping toward them.

The shadow went past them, colliding in a lethal dive with a lion that the boy hadn't even seen, camouflaged as it was against the stone. The shadow straightened up, a tall, dark skinned man with wings the colour of the plums that had grown in the orchard. Outlined by the sun, it was hard to see his face, but the boy did his best to meet the Avian's eyes squarely. If he died, he would do so with dignity.

The Avian's stance softened. "Della, Meri, it's all right. Come, boy, I'll show you how to skin and cook a lion."

Two more shadows landed, young women, one dark and the other colourful. They picked up the smallest of the band, the youngest children ready to fall where they stood, and glided to the caves. Soaring back, the colourful girl smiled at him. "You've done well, to bring them so far. What is your name?"

The boy fought back tears again. His name belonged to a happy young boy, with parents and a home. That boy was no more. "Owain, formerly of Noorinia. We're all that's left."

For now, at least. One day, he would return to his oasis home, and he would make the people who drove him out pay.

The tall Avian laid a hand on his shoulder. "I'm Mas, and these are my daughters. You may stay with us until you choose otherwise."

Chapter One

"Anee, come away from there!"

Owain looked up from his book on tactics, one of many Mas had him studying, just in time to scoop up his little brother as the toddler ran past, giggling.

Meri, the younger of the Avian sisters, who had taken on the care of the youngest children, swooped down a few seconds later, folding her arms. It was an interesting sight, in tandem with tucking her dark-green wings in, but the expression on Meri's face suggested that Owain might be wiser to hold off on making such an observation. She sat down next to him, clearly glad for a chance to rest. "How does a two year old move that fast? He literally just started walking!"

Owain could only shrug; Anee was the son of his father's second wife, and he didn't have much experience with young children. After all,

Owain was only twelve years older than his half-brother, what did he know about parenting? Father would have known what to do, or even Owain's older brother Fee, but both had died when Noorinia was invaded. Owain leaned into her, or more accurately, into the shade provided by her emerald green wings. "Thank you for looking after them."

There hadn't been time to search for all the children; only to shout for the ones nearest to him to stay close as he led them out into the desert. They had been re-creating the battle between the gods, where the wise god-king struck down his usurper brother -- The irony that Noorinia was betrayed and invaded by a supposed new ally, on the festival celebrating the triumph of good over evil was not lost on him -- while most of the girl-children had been doing... something else somewhere else. The girls who had been play-fighting alongside him were those who had little knowledge or experience with childrearing.

Meri waved a hand. "You were in need of help. Father wouldn't have turned any child away, and your people helped him, when he was learning."

It had been something of a shock, learning that the Avian warrior, Mas, was Della and Meri's primary parent, especially when Della was the only one who shared his colouring. According to everything Owain had read on Avians, males had very little to do with child-rearing, and chicks and fledglings were raised communally by a larger flock until they were ready to strike out on their own. Of course, it would hardly be the first surprise in the two months they had sheltered in the network of caves hidden within the rock formations.

Owain desperately wanted to know what had happened to bring about the unusual make-up of the tiny flock, but didn't think that it would be polite to ask. Instead, he focussed on the other part of her statement. "My people helped?

I don't remember any Avians coming to Noorinia."

She smiled, "You wouldn't; it was before you were born. We're long-lived, so we don't actually mate or have nestlings often. Della's mother fell afoul of hunters shortly before she hatched, so father returned here, and asked the advice of humans who raised nestlings. I think your father helped, since he'd just lost the woman he'd hoped to make his wife, and she'd left a son, who her family insisted he had no right to. Something about children following the mother?"

Ouch. So that was what happened to the oldest brother that Fee had only whispered stories about, and his father had refused to speak of. Children born before the wedding could be legitimised, if both parents consented, but if the mother or her family refused, that was an end to it. Owain tried to push away the stab of pain at the mention of his father, and the ideal of someone being left to show him how to lead.

Maybe Meri would have advice on how to deal with the loss. "What about your mother?"

Meri lifted her chin proudly. "Lord Mal, the same one who betrayed you, wanted Avian Nestlings for his collection of "exotics", to show that there was no-one he could not conquer. My mother died stopping his forces from gaining access to the Nesting Ground. Father and a few other warriors heard the commotion, and finished them off. He was the only survivor, but none of the invaders returned to their homes, either."

There was an old pain in Meri's voice, too, but also pride in the mother she barely remembered, and a refusal to diminish her actions by regretting them. Perhaps that was a path to healing; Owain would have to think on it.

She changed the topic, scooping up Anee and scrubbing him down with a soapy cloth, despite his yowls of protest. Water was scarce in the desert, which Anee viewed as a perfect reason that he should not have to wash every day, a sentiment shared by every child who disliked bath time. Their caretakers disagreed, and while actual baths were a luxury reserved for the Holy days, being washed was a daily requirement. "What are you studying?"

Owain rubbed his forehead, "Tactics, and some of the reports Mas gathered on what happened to the survivors. Once he thinks we're ready, we're going to start rescuing them."

It was an intimidating prospect, at least to Owain's mind, but at least they weren't alone; Mas might be the most intimidating individual Owain had ever encountered, but he was one of the most impressive warriors Owain had ever seen, and an excellent teacher. He wouldn't let them go out until he thought that they *were* ready. Owain knew that it wasn't possible to become a capable warrior in only a few weeks, but he wished there was a way to hurry the process. The longer they delayed, the more his people suffered.

Meri bit her lip, "Come talk to Della and me when you start making concrete plans. There are a few things that you and Father may not have considered."

*   *   *

Owain tried not to flinch as blades clashed and sand was kicked up by rapid feet as he dodged a blow. He was not in Noorinia, Lord Mal's soldiers were not trying to kill him. He forced himself out of the nightmare and blocked the next strike, sliding away and spinning around to level his sword at Mas's chest.

The warrior stepped back, lowering his sword, and graced Owain with a rare smile. "Well done. You are ready."

Owain tried not to beam; it had taken two years to get to this point, on top of his already formidable skills, but he had done it. Off to the side, Gerin cheered loudly. Mas ignored him. "Now, you need to make sure the ones you take with you are also ready, and come up with a plan."

Owain nodded, trying not to panic at the thought of actually leading a mission. "About that, Della and Meri had some things they want to talk to us about."

Mas raised an eyebrow, but nodded, gesturing for the others to keep practicing. They walked to the large tent where the younger children gathered, and where Della and Meri spent most of the day, when they weren't taking turns hunting.

Owain tried not to watch when Meri hunted, not so much due to squeamishness, but because Meri in a killing dive was a glorious sight that did unfamiliar things to his anatomy. Not necessarily unpleasant things, but potentially embarrassing. Also potentially dangerous, if Mas's protective tendencies became an issue.

Thankfully, it was Della - brisk, compassionate and very good at ignoring what someone didn't want to talk about - who sat down with them. She didn't waste time. "One of the warriors you take with you has to be female, and you need to consider potential living arrangements once they have arrived."

Owain was always willing to have someone explain things he was ignorant about. "I do not disagree with you, but could you please elaborate?"

There was a brief silence as Della searched for the words. "The life of one in bondage is not easy. You will have women who cannot bear the presence of men, and men who are uneasy in the company of women. Wounds of the mind and soul scar just as deeply as those of the body, and can be harder to heal."

Mas closed his eyes, both in regret and clearly blaming himself for the oversight. "I should have considered that. Thank you, my heart."

Owain nodded seriously. Della was undoubtedly talking about more than the sick, heartrending grief of losing his home and his family, the flashbacks that he had worked so hard to overcome... but that had been hard enough in its own right. He should have realised that those who had been enslaved would have it much worse. "We have the space for separate living areas, though they will still have to share with others. Do we know anyone with a gift for mind healing who can be trusted?"

Della shook her head, "Just me, and I'm far from an expert. I'll help to the best of my abilities, and see if anyone from the nearest flocks can be trusted, but I can make no promises."

Owain relaxed a little; some help was better than none. "Thank you, Della. We'll go ahead with the plan, and work the rest out later."

Chapter Two

Owain was starting to understand what Mas meant when he said that no plan survived the first five minutes of being put into action. ["No Plan survives contact with the enemy." – Sun Tzu, *The Art of War*. But of course you can't quote that.]

Oh, they'd got into the city easily enough, disguised as a slave trader looking to buy, and his guards, and confirmed the presence of the former Noorinans they were looking for. They had even managed to make contact with at least one in each of the Houses where they were kept. That was when the problems had started.

Several of Owain's people had proven 'uncooperative' and been sold on to the Arena. Those that remained within easier reach flatly refused to leave the other unwilling inhabitants behind, even if it imperilled their own chances of escape. It wasn't a sentiment that Owain could really disagree with, even if he had wanted to, but it did make re-evaluating their plans infinitely more difficult.

The resources of their desert sanctuary were scarce, and while the Avian flock were working on expanding those resources, there was currently no way to support the hundreds of slaves in just this city. Then, of course, there was the bit where it would be impossible to take that many slaves out without far too many questions and scrutiny. A dozen or so, yes, a slaver and two guards could be expected to manage that many, but hundreds?

Oh, this was a disaster! His first mission, and Owain was already proving himself a failure. He was supposed to protect his people, and he couldn't even free a handful of them from bondage!

The door burst open, and Gerin burst in, looking both elated and furious as he dropped into the free chair. Owain glanced up, fingers still gripping his hair. "I suppose you had the same problem I did?"

Gerin scowled. "I found Banti. She says that she's not going anywhere unless we bring the others, too."

Siria, one of the few girls who had been with Owain when they escaped the sacking of their home, stalked in on Gerin's heels, blood on her knuckles and in a towering fury. Owain winced; he had no doubt that whoever Siria had left bleeding had richly deserved it, but they were trying *not* to draw attention. He didn't even need to raise an eyebrow before Siria burst out, "That bitch told me that if I ever wanted to stop pretending to be a warrior, she'd have a job for me!"

Owain winced again. "Please tell me you didn't punch the Madam. We may actually need to get back in there one day."

Siria shook her head, "No, I punched the lout who assumed that I would agree and tried to get handsy. Then the Bouncer offered me a job."

That... might be useful, if they ever needed someone to go undercover. Owain put that idea to the side for now. "So, we have multiple problems and no clear solutions. Tell me your thoughts."

Siria groaned, the rage draining from her like water from a jug. "We can't free everyone at once. I hate the idea of leaving a single soul behind, but there are only three of us. We can't liberate an entire city by ourselves."

Her words sparked a potential idea, but he needed to think on it more first. "Gerin?"

His oldest friend shook his darker head. "We can't target more than one place, or we risk spreading ourselves too thin, or worse, tipping off owners who could happily kill their stock and start over, rather than let us free them."

It wasn't nice to hear his own worries confirmed, but something in Owain's chest eased anyway. "We also can't support that many new people in our sanctuary, either. Not yet. So, the question becomes thus; which target can we reasonably liberate, and which should be our priority?"

Gerin dropped his head into his hands. "Every part of me wants to kick the shit out of the place holding Banti, but the Houses at least have a vested interest in keeping their stock alive and unbroken, and a minimum age requirement. As much as I hate it, they're as well-off as they can be there."

Siria's voice was as sympathetic as her brusque nature ever got. "The Arena. It has the highest mortality rate, and an increased chance of survival if we have to fight our way out."

Pride was one of Siria's flaws, and there was no easy way to admit that they were severely lacking in the number of people capable of holding their own in a fight. Still... Owain had one reservation. "Volunteers only. We don't trade on gratitude."

*   *   *

Anee's nurse had been a freed slave, and her voice drifted across Owain's mind. "*There are a hundred ways to be enslaved. They don't have to be named to be true.*"

It would be the worst of crimes to free the Arena fighters, only to force them to fight again, regardless of the cause. His companions nodded, seeing the same logic, and Owain relaxed. "Get some rest, both of you. I'll let Mas know what's going on.

Gerin and Siria happily collapsed on the two beds in the room; the day had been even more emotionally draining than physically. Owain dearly wanted to do the same on the lumpy chair, but delayed in favour of pulling a small orb out of his belt pouch. It was magical, if a touch limited in its power, and allowed the user to speak over distance. He activated it, and a deep voice answered almost immediately. "Owain?"

Owain kept his voice soft, both to avoid waking his companions and to make things harder for any eavesdroppers powerful enough to get around the wards that came with the room. Explaining the situation took far less time than he expected, and he could almost envision Mas nodding thoughtfully. "What do you plan to do?"

Owain tried to keep the emotion out of his voice. It was harder than he had expected. "We're going to investigate the Arena, and try to stage a raid there. They'll be either fighters, or slaves that were willing to fight back and were sentenced as killing fodder for the Gladiators."

Mas paused to consider before he replied, "Have you considered that the Arena will be more secure?"

Owain had, but was trying not to borrow trouble by panicking about it. "Yes, that's why we're investigating, first. With luck, there will be a few willing to rise up if the time comes."

There was a trace of warmth in his mentor's normally-impassive voice. "Good. You have the charm I taught you. Contact me when you make your plans."

Noorinia had boasted a high number of people able to perform magic, Owain's family among them, though rarely at a level high enough to be sought as Magicians. The ability to predict sandstorms, keep rats and insects out of stores, find water, or the occasional brief vision... that was the most Owain had ever seen.

The charm Mas had taught him was a basic one, and barely legal. Able to magically disarm and remove the marks that killed a slave who attempted to escape, it could be performed by anyone with a basic level of magic, but their use was highly regulated, and punishable by heavy fines and imprisonment.

Of course, such potential punishments were the least of Owain's problems if they were caught, and the stakes were high enough to be worth it.

*   *   *

Their disguises did not need many adjustments to turn them from slavers to nomads, and Owain was good at going un-noticed.

It was common for visitors to the city to wander through the pens, 'examining the goods' before placing bets on the outcome, and they split up, wandering through and taking in every possible detail. The exits were surprisingly loosely guarded, though with the collars, perhaps that was understandable. A passage led to a guardroom, though not as heavily staffed as it could have been.

Then again, was an excess of guards really needed, when you could literally kill any potential uprising with a word? Lost in thought and half-formed plans, Owain managed not to jump when a hand reached through the bars to grab his wrist. "You really came."

The speaker was a tall man, perhaps a handful of years older than Owain himself, tattoos etched in gold across his cheeks, with the muscles and scars that indicated a trained, long-term gladiator. Owain frowned; he didn't recognise him, and now was a bad time to trust blindly. "Do I know you?"

The man grinned, cocky and irreverent. "No, but I saw you coming."

The emphasis on the word, and the glimmer of silver that surrounded the man like dust motes, invisible to the majority of the population, made Owain look more closely at the tattoos. "You're a Seer."

The man nodded. "Quinn, last of the Kir, thanks to a certain Warlord that you are unfortunately familiar with. I saw that, too, and I'm sorry for your loss, but not sorry that it eventually led you here."

Owain winced; memories of that night would never truly fade, but he knew that Seers were merely the messengers, and not to blame for what they saw. "Did you see anything else?"

Quinn shrugged. "Myself at your side, but nothing to state when or where. Only that you would come, and your intent."

Damn. Reassurance of success would have been nice, but having someone able to vouch for him among the Gladiators was nothing to scoff at. Quinn's eyes flickered to the side, to a guard that was paying a little too much attention. "Look like you're inspecting me."

Owain ran his hand down one arm, trying not to notice the lean, hard muscles too much. Ugh, if his hormones could hurry up and stabilise, his life would be much easier. The guard relaxed, stalking over to someone else who was getting a little too familiar. Owain lifted Quinn's chin, tilting his head from side to side. "Then, will you help us?"

Quinn's eyes were hopeful but cautious, hard experience making him wary of trusting anyone without suspecting ulterior motives. "For how long?"

Owain shrugged, "Until we get you out of here, then for as little or as long as suits you."

The gladiator beamed, fierce and vengeful. "Then you can count on me. What do you need?"

Owain bit his lip, then took a risk, murmuring the spell to free Quinn. "Gather those you know you can trust, and be ready. Try and protect the kill fodder as much as you can; we hope to strike tomorrow."

Quinn nodded seriously, and gripped Owain's arm in a warrior's clasp. "I await your word."

*   *   *

The next day's battle was a Grand Melee, which made Owain very grateful that he had chosen not to wait.

Grand Melees were fought not between small groups until only one was left, but between large numbers, with everyone for themselves until a timer ran out. It would be a massacre on a grand scale, and as long as Owain drew breath, he would do his utmost to never witness such a thing again.

Gerin was in the crowd, Siria slipping into the pens to free those few not involved and deal with the guards. Mas had arrived in the dark of pre-dawn, in case they needed back-up or just support in escaping the actual city. Owain had wanted to succeed on his own merit, but couldn't deny that they were likely to need the help. He wouldn't let his own pride ruin their chances.

The crowds cheered for their favourites as the day's chosen entertainment walked into the Arena. Hidden in the shadows, Owain slipped into their ranks, moving up until he stood beside Quinn, other gladiators gathering around with varying degrees of subtlety. "As soon as they start the games, we head for the exit."

The noise of the crowd was like a sledgehammer to his ears, but it made a good cover. With all the shouting, no-one was going to hear him or Gerin whispering the spell, even if they were standing right next to them. Among the kill fodder, largely composed of Noorinian captives, Owain caught more than a few startled glances as they recognised him.

Finally, the shouting subsided, and the announcer raised a brightly coloured cloth, holding over the balcony. "When this touches the sand, to death or countdown, let the battle commence!"

The cloth fluttered down, and Quinn raised his sword, as if in salute. "Shields up, fan out!"

The gladiators near him ran to surround the other captives, raising their shields. The slave marks also stifled any active use of magic, and there were panicked shouts as magical barriers flowed from the raised shields, overlapping to protect everyone from anything the guards atop the walls could use at a distance.

One of the doors began to open, and Owain saw Siria, holding off a handful of guards while the remainder of the captives kept the doors from closing. He pointed, "There!"

Quinn's face shone, and he raised his sword. "Ram formation! To freedom!"

The crowd started to panic, the confusion making it doubly hard for the guards to act. Gerin dropped down, running to join them as the gladiators formed columns, still keeping the barriers up, and took off at a run toward the doors. Siria jumped out of the way as they ploughed into and over the guards, then led the last of the pens' occupants behind them as they flowed out into the sunlight.

Chapter Three

Their flight from the Arena to the desert Sanctuary was a journey of days.

About half of their initial number of rescues had branched off early, seeking their own homes and families, or planning to stay and create safehouses for future freedom efforts. A few of the gladiators intended to use their freedom and the town's sudden lack of fighters to get paid for the work that they did best. A few merely rejected the thought of living in the desert.

That still left a few dozen for Owain to protect as they fled, thanking the fates for Banti's water-sense. Gerin's shouting had been... memorable, when he discovered that she had been sent to join the kill fodder the very morning of the break-out. Owain was just thankful that Banti had mouthed off enough times that her transfer happened before the attack, rather than after they left. Banti was a gentle soul, and wouldn't have survived until their return.

The rock formations were finally within sight, a distant figure circling overhead, and it was so tempting to relax, to luxuriate in the feeling of safety. Owain wanted to rest, but didn't dare drop his guard, some sixth sense warning him that they were not safe yet.

Darkness swirled ahead of them, blacker even than shadows, and a band of armed guards suddenly appeared, surrounding a ragged figure weighed down by chains. The figure promptly slumped to the ground, still and unmoving, and the guards paid him no notice. Instead, they charged toward the weary band making their way to safety.

Mas was a fearsome warrior, but even he had his limits, and shepherding the former captives through the desert with little rest had taken its toll. Three guards met their fate at his hand, several more falling to Owain, Siri, Quinn and Gerin, before sheer numbers started to overwhelm them. Even Mas began to falter, and Owain tried not to panic.

The majority of the freed prisoners also suffered battle-weariness, as Owain had, obedience to guards beaten into them over years. Most of them cowered, or tried to flee. Owain didn't blame them, but he raged inside. They were so close to freedom and safety! They couldn't fail now!

A sound like the scream of an eagle split the air, and a flash of green plummeted through the air, striking the Guard Commander with a sickening crack. He dropped like a stone, neck lolling at an impossible angle, and Meri whirled, her eyes like green fire as a beat of her powerful wings drove sand into their attackers' eyes. A kick from taloned feet drew a deep gash over another's neck, and he fell back, clutching his throat as blood spilled from between his fingers.

Owain took advantage of the distraction to pull Quinn and the few others who had stayed to fight into a semblance of a defensive formation. Black and indigo swooped in from another direction, guards sent flying as Della flew low enough for her wings to impact heads and chests at high speed, before rising out of reach and flying after the fleeing former prisoners. If any other guards had followed them, they would need to assistance.

A guard who started to force the survivors back into formation screamed as Meri's talons dug into his shoulders and arms, carrying him high into the air before letting him fall. If he survived the fall, he wouldn't survive the lack of immediate medical intervention. Mas began to do the same, sending the remainder into disarray, making them far easier targets as the warrior flew after his elder daughter.

Siria ran to examine the chained figure, who hadn't so much as twitched, despite the battle raging around them. Owain beheaded the last guard, and shot her a questioning look. Siri shook her head. "Dead. The ability to transport others is rare, and taxing at the best of times. Bringing so many must have done him in."

Mas landed beside them, making Quinn jump (and instantly try to pretend that he had done no such thing). "We will bury him. Leave the others to the jackals and vultures."

Meri circled above them before hovering awkwardly, trying to re-wrap her feet in mid-air before touching down on the hot sand. Owain knew better than to laugh, and also knew better than to actually say how incredibly attracted to the Avian girl he was. Watching Meri hunt had paled in comparison to how glorious she looked in a fight.

Hastily, he busied himself with organising their rescued prisoners for the final leg. Adolescent imaginings could wait until later.

*　　*　　*

Owain was a young man, being propositioned by an attractive young woman that he considered a close and very dear friend. She needed someone to help her through her first reproductive cycle (something Avians viewed with an odd practicality, given how intense and infrequent it apparently was, given the almost-decade between Della and Meri), and it didn't have to be anything more than they both wanted it to be.

(*Hormones outweighed the consideration of exactly how Mas was likely to react when he discovered Owain's involvement with his precious younger daughter. That was a panic attack for later, when Meri wasn't waiting for his answer.*)

He stood up, smiling as he took her hand and attempting to flirt like Quinn did. "You do realise that I can't fly?"

Meri beamed at him, so he must be doing something right. "No, but you do have a very aerial-based fighting style. We can adapt."

It was half flight, half dance, graceful and enthralling and potentially deadly. Avian flight was even more glorious when Meri used her momentum to lift him into the air, deadly talons grasping without piercing his skin, and he hung, weightless, for several seconds, until she caught him again and set him down gently. Hearts pounding and blood on fire with adrenaline and lust, Owain didn't know which one of them reached for the other first.

*　　*　　*

Later, Owain would kick himself for expecting Avian reproduction to be identical to a human pregnancy. They might share many characteristics, but Avians were, at the heart of it, just as bird-like as they were human-inclined. The main difference was that Avians were incredibly fertile during their extremely limited mating cycles, far more so than humans.

Owain's romance with Meri had been no more than a fling, as he suspected, and he was just as happy to remain her close friend. The fact that their relationship didn't last was no reason to expect that there would be no consequences, however. He really shouldn't be surprised at the result, and the way Mas was glaring at him should probably be of greater concern.

Still, an *egg*?

Meri was smirking at his clear shock, while Della and Banti giggled in the background. Owain shot the girl who was his little sister as much as Gerin's a quelling look, which Banti ignored. He focused on his former lover. "Do you need to nest on it, like birds do?"

Meri shook her head. "No, just keep it warm, and talk to the chick. Traditionally, Avian women rear the children, but she should know her father."

A daughter. Owain's mind was filled with a vision of a tiny child, fluttering after him on clumsy wings, or toddling as Anee had. Would she have wings, being only half-Avian? Would she inherit his father's eyes, like Owain and the rest of his family did? Owain might be young to be a father, but they were already all-but-raising

Anee together, even if their relationship was only that of friends.

He forced himself to focus. "I'm not Avian, and Mas did a good job of caring for you. I'll be as involved as you let me."

Apparently, it was the right answer, because Mas's fiery glare, which had been giving Owain a prickle between his shoulder blades (not unlike the sixth sense when someone was about to try to stab him) for the last hour, lessened, and Meri smiled, the same beaming joy he had first been attracted to. "Good."

*　　*　　*

Of course, the egg was a product of him and Meri, so naturally it was never going to do things the easy way.

Owain bolted upright in the middle of the night at the sound of a loud 'crack'. The silence from outside allowed him to relax; it was not an attack. Then he looked at the egg, nestled between his and Meri's bedrolls in blankets spelled to be a consistent warm temperature. A large crack was spreading over the shell, and it had nearly rocked itself out of the little nest that cradled it.

He threw off his blankets, shaking Meri, who instantly came alert. She began to croon at the egg, murmuring a stream of encouragement, and gestured for him to go fetch her father and sister. Owain left at a run, somehow collecting Gerin and Anee along the way.

Mas and Della had the advantage of flight, and not having to dodge around tents and firepits. (Their numbers had expanded beyond the capacity of the caves to hold, so the less vulnerable slept outside) By the time Owain got back, they were standing against the walls of the tent, singing softly in the Avian tongue.

The cracks on the egg were spreading, and a large piece broke away, a tiny face poking out. It retreated just as quickly, and Meri reached out to stop him when he would have pulled away other pieces. "No, she is only resting. Breaking the shell is hard work, but she must do it herself."

Owain forced himself to relax. "It's all right, little one. Your mother and I will be here when you are ready. Take as long as you need."

It took nearly an hour, small pieces falling to enlarge the original hole, and an expression of well-hidden concern had started to appear on Mas's face when the shell split cleanly in half, and a fair-skinned infant, blue-grey eyes touched with a hint of Meri's piercing green and a damp tuft of orange and gold feathers at her back, appeared, loudly expressing her displeasure at the situation with a piercing trill.

Owain picked her up, small enough to fit in his cupped hands, and gently towelled her dry. "She's so small."

Mas's voice was dry, but affectionate. "She'll grow, and faster than you expect."

He knelt down, producing a bowl of mashed... something, and handing it to Meri, who tipped

a small amount into the baby's open mouth.
Mas stood, following Della out the door. "Spend
the day with your daughter; we will take care of
things."

Gerin, Anee, Quinn and Banti, the latter two
having arrived un-noticed, crowded around in
curiosity. Mas's usual brusque tones returned.
"The rest of you, out! She needs two parents,
not an entire flock!"

They scattered, and Meri laughed, giving the
baby another mouthful. Owain gazed down at
the tiny face, recognising his own nose and
cheekbones, along with his father's eyes. "What
is her name?"

That, at least, was the prerogative of the mother,
in both of their cultures. Meri smiled, radiating
the wonder and adoration that Owain was
certain reflected in his own face. "Lyssi. It
means perseverance, and a promise for the
future."

Owain smiled, silver edging his vision as he saw a girl, golden-red hair like his own, standing fierce and proud and defiant, as though daring the world to stop her. The silver, and the Vision of the future, faded, and he stroked the currently-fair wisps on Lyssi's head. "It suits her."

Chapter Four

The raid on the Arena had been followed by two more in the last year, still targeting the places that held Noorinia's survivors. Della and Meri were joined by several others, both male and female, who were happy to help raise the numerous children, whether those children were Noorinian or 'orphaned' former slaves. Now, it was time to work out the longer-term plans.

Owain sat with Mas as they smoked and dried meat from their latest hunt, several miles away from the sanctuary. Mas looked up at the sky, "Have you thought about what you will do now?"

Owain had thought of little but. "I want to try and re-unite what is left of my people. It may not be possible, but I want to find the ones we can, and avenge the ones we can't."

Mas looked at him approvingly, carving another joint to be dried into jerky. "What of your long-term plans?"

That would be even more difficult than their current crusade of freeing slaves. That didn't make Owain any less determined. "I want to take back my home. We can't do it now, Lord Mal will be on the alert for such things, and we don't have the ability to mount so much as an incursion. I... hoped that you might have a suggestion or two."

Mas stood up and clapped him on the shoulder. "Become mercenaries. You will learn skills and make connections that will be of use to you later. Noorinia is of immense value; Lord Mal will find that keeping what he stole will be harder than taking it. When you have established a reputation, you may be contracted to help besiege your old home, and you can use that time to gather intelligence."

The thought of leaving Mal to enjoy Noorinia as spoils made Owain want to punch something, but his mentor was correct. They had to be smart about this. "You were a mercenary once, I think? Can you teach me what I need to be successful, and any of the others who will follow?"

Mas's smiles had frequently been called terrifying by those who didn't know him, but Owain had mostly grown out of the habit of flinching at the sight of bared teeth. "Gladly."

*   *   *

Quinn, Siria and Gerin had agreed in a heartbeat, as had the rest of the youths Mas had already helped train. Some of the freed captives were leaning toward joining them, but needed time to think it over. A few were still getting used to the ability to make decisions at all, and Owain had no intention of approaching them until they had more confidence.

Quinn lingered after the others left, clearly wanting a private word, and Owain resigned himself to a missed meal. "What troubles you? Another vision?"

Quinn shook his head. "Yes and no. When I was taken, there was another, an Avian youth, who helped me survive until I could take care of myself. He was sold on about a week before you came."

There weren't many reasons why Quinn would bring that up, and he seemed unusually urgent. Owain's brow furrowed. "You want us to find him?"

His friend nodded. "I had a vision. If we don't get him out, he doesn't live past a month longer. I owe him everything, so if you don't think it's worth the risk, I'm informing you of my temporary absence while I make the attempt."

Quinn rushing off, unprepared and unaccompanied, was the last thing anyone needed, the seer himself included. Owain held up his hands. "Try and pinpoint his location, and we'll head there as soon as I can get things organised."

*   *   *

Meri, accompanied by a few of the freed women, managed to corner him before they left. Lyssi wasn't fluttering behind her, so this was a serious talk. "Your plan to become mercenaries... there is more to consider."

Owain paused in his study of the city lay-out, giving her his full attention. "Go on."

Meri sat down beside her father, folding her wings. "Several of the freed asked me about learning to fight. Not in combat, but to defend themselves and those too young or traumatised to fight back if attacked. It would free you up from leaving a guard every time you go on missions, and be good for their confidence."

Owain glanced at Mas, who gave the idea serious consideration. "We would be more effective if we didn't have to leave half our force behind all the time."

Meri smiled, but Owain caught the glint in her eye that said she was about to dig her heels in about something. He braced himself for something that he or Mas or both of them were not going to like. "Della and I are already leading them, in a sense, and it would be even easier if you helped refine my skills."

As expected, Mas did not take that nearly as well, which was probably why Meri had tried to slip it in without notice. Also as expected, Meri proved that she was just as capable of digging her heels in as her father was. Finally, Owain intervened. "Put Siria in charge for now, and we'll re-visit the issue when we return."

*   *   *

Several set-backs while travelling meant that they didn't have nearly as much time to scout the city as Owain would have liked. Relying heavily on Quinn's visions, Owain and his band found themselves watching a glorified training session. Quinn's Avian friend was blond, his hair in a single braid, rather than the many dark braids that Mas and his daughters favoured. His wings were a striking blue, like the desert flowers that sprung up in the brief wet season.

Brek, descended from the Lizardmen who lived in the heart of the desert and one of their newer recruits, frowned as he watched. "Why doesn't he fly? It would make it much easier for him to dodge."

Owain and Quinn looked closer, before Quinn swore viciously. Owain explained for the benefit of the others, after Quinn proved that he wasn't going to run out of profanity or breath any time soon. "Look at his wings; the primary feathers are broken. He can't get properly airborne, and I doubt he could manage more than a short glide without more pain and energy that it's worth."

There was a long moment of silence. The small band was familiar enough with Avians to know how the loss of flight must affect the warrior. Still, perhaps it could be healed... "For the Gods sake, Quinn, stop swearing! You're drawing too much attention!"

Quinn lowered his voice, at least, though he kept up a steady stream of dire imprecations, each more creative than the last. Finally, their moment came. Guards entered the ring to bring the gladiators (thankfully today was just an exhibition, rather than a killing match) back to their cells.

One guard prodded the tall Avian... and promptly slumped to the ground, Owain's keen eyes picking out a dart embedded in his back. Not at all up to Quinn's usual accuracy, but under the circumstances, it was understandable. The guards turned to face the new threat as Owain raised his sword and followed Quinn in vaulting over the barrier and into the Arena. Quinn's anger was more than justified, but it made him reckless, just enough that a guard managed to get past his defence and knock him to the ground. Owain killed his current opponent with a vicious back-cut, but knew he wouldn't get to Quinn in time. With a roar, he attacked anyway; he would not watch another friend die.

Fortunately, he didn't have to. A powerful gust of wind knocked the guard off-balance, the weapon falling from his hand. Quinn rolled out of the way and dispatched his attacker. "Thanks, Khi."

'Khi' pulled him upright, his face a mask of pain as he folded his wings again, "It's Khial, you pest. Don't thank me just yet."

His voice had a musical lilt to it, putting Owain more in mind of a songbird than the harsher, raptor-like tones of Mas's family. He took care of the last of the guards. "Why not?"

Khial gestured to the doorway. "Because they brought help. We're not safe yet."

Owain swore, borrowing a few examples from Quinn, as an entire troop marched through. Unlike the bullying toughs that made up the Arena guard, these were trained professionals. Owain touched the orb in his belt pouch, hoping that Mas was paying attention to its counterpart.

The captain of the reinforcements, unfortunately and sensibly, was staying firmly behind a barrier of his troops as he shouted orders. That was only a defence from ground attacks, however, and Owain had back up of his own. A javelin flashed out of the sky and struck the captain squarely in the torso. The added momentum of an Avian plummet drove it straight through his body, pinning him to the sand.

A flash of tan and emerald followed a moment later, a sickening *crunch* giving the soldiers pause as Meri used one of their number as a springboard, launching herself back into the air. A curved blade scythed through two more, before spinning back up for Mas to catch.

Wonder and longing almost replaced the pain on Khial's face as he stared up at the two Avians, now circling around for another attack. Had he ever seen another Avian in full flight, or had it just been so long that he had forgotten? If Quinn was correct about Khial's origins, perhaps he hadn't. "Who is *that*?"

Owain recognised the expression on Khial's face, as well as the tone of voice. He had worn it himself, not so long ago, and Khial had probably never seen the full extent of an Avian battle (Mas was defending the perimeter, keeping reinforcements from reaching the Guards). Meri had an admirer, it seemed. Della seemed happy enough without a mate, and insisted that if she ever took one she would follow the traditional route, but Khial had been raised in captivity, socialised in the experiences of human bonds. Owain wondered how that would affect his attitude toward relationships.

They won, but not without taking a certain amount of damage. Quinn's mild concussion was going to make the next few days deeply unpleasant, but might get him out of more than a severe scolding from Mas about keeping his focus in combat. Owain had a cut that probably wouldn't require stitches, just bandaging, and everyone else sported only minor injuries that would heal on their own within a week.

The other two Avians alighted softly on the Arena sands, Meri shooting her father 'I-told-you-so' looks. Owain wasn't sure that it would help her case for further combat instruction, but he certainly wasn't about to involve himself in that particular family spat. Meri smiled brightly at Khial, her expression turning to horrified fury when she saw his wings. "Who did that to you, and are they still alive for me to kill slowly?"

Mas sighed in exasperation, but pointedly didn't disagree with his daughter's unusually-aggressive stance. Khial shrugged, "I lost count a long time ago, honestly."

Owain could hear a lot of grinding teeth, and didn't blame them. Still, he tried to get everyone back on track. "We need to leave before more reinforcements show up. Come on, all of you."

Khial shook his head. "You take the others, but I have to stay. There's a new batch due to arrive tomorrow, and they won't have anyone to help them if I leave."

Owain glanced at Quinn, who looked ready to object, likely at volume, and then to a thoughtful Meri. "Do you have a plan?"

Khial nodded, "I've been in the area long enough to have made contact with the Underground. I'll join you once I've organised things here."

Meri stepped forward. "I'll stay with you, if you don't mind. At the very least, I can take a stab at healing you."

Khial gave her a measuring look, but nodded, and Owain tried not to think of all the things that could go wrong as he led the others away.

Chapter Five

Owain didn't relax until Meri and Khial returned three weeks later, with a dozen freed captives, news of the beginnings of an underground network, and a surprise.

A displeased Mas was something that Owain made a point of avoiding. His daughters - and, it seemed, Khial - did not share that concern. In fact, Della was trying and failing to hold back a fit of giggles as Mas scowled at his younger daughter and, apparently, her new husband.

Meri looked exasperated, despite being pinned with a glare that could - and had - sent most beings running. "Father, don't you think you're over-reacting?"

Mas scowled, "It was a simple undercover mission - that was *not* a euphemism, Della, stop *laughing*! - to gather intelligence. How did you manage to come back from it married?"

Lyssi, who was at a stage where she mimicked the adults around her, giggled along with Della. Owain plucked her out of the air, musing that a third person couldn't be a bad thing when it came to looking after his tiny bundle of energy. Quinn and Gerin both bolted to a distance where they could hear, but were out of direct sight; Owain hoped that they would actually get out of earshot before they started laughing.

Meri did not share their sense of self-preservation. "People pay less attention to a married couple. It was a good cover."

Khial took her hand. "Then there were witnesses who saw Meri tending to my wings, and some of them actually knew what that meant. Afterward, we decided that it would be too much fuss to get a divorce."

Mas threw up his hands and stalked away, and Owain decided that the whole mess was going on the list of things that were Not His Problem To Deal With. He had too many things that were his problem to go looking for more. One of which was the additional influx. "Meri, do you mind if I catch you up on what you've missed?"

She smiled at him, not letting go of Khial's hand. "Della looked strained; I take it that shelter is still an issue?"

He nodded, "We need to scout for either a larger location, or a second defensible shelter. Even with most of us sleeping in tents or in shifts, there just isn't enough room."

Khial cut in. "I have a suggestion, but it would involve re-locating."

Owain hoped that he didn't look as relieved as he felt. "I'm willing to hear it."

Khial tried to ignore Mas's piercing glare. "It is... it was my flock's ancestral nesting ground. In a few months, instinct will guide me. It will not be easy to get to, but it will be a safe haven for us."

Mas stopped glaring, and looked an odd mixture of impressed and concerned, which Owain thought was a rather unfair about-turn in attitude. "Are you sure? Nesting grounds are not intruded upon lightly."

Khial nodded. "I am the last of my flock. Better that we take shelter there, as part of a new flock, than that I allow it to be abandoned to ghosts."

Owain tried not to focus too hard on having to re-locate all of them to who-knew-where. "At least mountains are a bit more defensible, and harder to besiege."

Grief passed over Khial's face. "It's not impossible, but this time we will know to be on our guard, and from what I last heard, my flock's murderer has found himself a desert city to hole up in, so he, at least, will not come searching."

That... sounded a bit too familiar. "You're not talking about Mal, by any chance?"

Khial looked startled, then sympathetic. "Your home suffered the same fate."

Owain nodded, the memory of his father's corpse as fresh as the day it happened.

"Noorinia. That's where he's made his new home. One day, we'll take it back."

Khial clasped Owain's arm in a warrior's promise. "I'll be with you, and in the meantime, my home will be yours."

Mas interrupted them, back to his usual stern visage. "I suggest leaving a small force here, in case more of the newly-freed come."

It was a sensible suggestion, and several of their expanded settlement would struggle to adapt to the colder climate of the mountains. Owain nodded, "I'll talk to the ones who are more desert-adapted. With our numbers, it wouldn't be a terrible idea to split into smaller bands."

Quinn agreed with him. "We would have to anyway, at some point, if we decided to follow through with your idea of becoming mercenaries. A band for hire is one thing. A full army that answers to no-one and nowhere is something else entirely."

When Owain had first thought of becoming a mercenary band, their numbers had been only the few who had escaped the Massacre of Noorinia. A decent size for a company, even discounting those who didn't want to, or couldn't, fight. Their current numbers were too much for any one captain to handle. Several companies, who could join together under one leader when the time came... well, even Quinn came up with good ideas now and then. "I'll talk to some of the leaders and see who is willing to take command."

*　　*　　*

Siria had found enough female volunteers to form her own company, to Owain's minor concern (a company comprised solely of women would have a harder time getting most employers to take them seriously), leaving Meri to take over training those who preferred to defend the vulnerable rather than actively seek conflict.

Quinn had taken charge of a second company, with Brek as his second, in the hope that the Lizardman's cool rationality would balance Quinn's admittedly-deserved arrogance. Owain had chosen Gerin as his own second for a similar reason; he hoped that Gerin would become a Captain in his own right eventually, but he needed more experience in planning and logistics first.

Anee wasn't happy about Owain going away without him, and was making his displeasure generally known. While thankful that his little brother would miss him, Owain wished that he didn't have to be quite so public about it. A vocal, angry seven-year-old dogging his heels was exhausting. "Anee, you're still too young."

Anee scowled up at him. "But Mas says that I'm very advanced and a quick learner!"

Owain mentally apologised to his father, and to Mas, if he had ever been this block-headed. "You are, and I'm proud of you, but you're too young, and yes, I would say that to anyone, no matter their skill. I put in a minimum age requirement for a reason, and I will not make an exception for you."

Anee stamped his foot, lower lip quivering. "But what if you die and never come back? You don't care!"

Owain stopped, unable to refute that there was a risk, but didn't get the chance to say anything before Anee ran away from him, sand flying beneath his feet. A flutter of wings made him turn, relaxing as he met Meri's understanding gaze. "They all go through a stage like this, don't worry. Just make a point of coming back safe and well. I'll talk to him while you're away."

Owain smiled, and kissed Lyssi's bright curls. "Thank you. I'll see you again soon."

Chapter Six

'Be confident, but not arrogant.'

'Don't let them cheat or insult you with paying too little, but remember you can't command the same price as an experienced troupe.'

'Listen to the voices of experience, but don't be hesitant to speak up and be mindful of your troops' wellbeing.'

'Build a reputation, but be careful what that reputation is. Some will do anything for money, but you've seen where that leads. Draw a line, and refuse to cross it.'

'Become who you need to be, but don't let it change who you are.'

Owain had been Captain of his Mercenary Band for six months, and he still repeated the advice he had been given over and over in his mind. They had done small jobs, so far - guarding merchants and wealthy families, acting as scouts for larger war-bands, and the like - but they had already received a few letters of recommendation for being good at what they did. There was only one type of job they had refused; anything involving the conveyance or re-capture of slaves.

That job, Owain had taken careful note of the details, and sent word to Meri and Siria. Last he heard, the trip had proven most unprofitable for the Slavers. Fatal, even, for several of them, which Owain considered a bonus.

Of course, it would be only a matter of time before word got around and Slavers stopped approaching him at all, but Khial said that the Freedom Trail were working on getting agents into place for the same purpose.

The current job was guarding a supply train to the army currently besieging Noorinia, which accounted for Owain's current nerves. It had been almost six years since he had seen his home, even from a distance, yet the memories still lurked vivid in the back of his mind. Owain inhaled deeply through his nose and breathed out through his mouth, doing his best to push the memories away. The last thing he needed was to gain a reputation for flashbacks.

To distract himself, he studied the landscape. Noorinia had been built around an oasis, sheltered from the worst of the desert sandstorms by a rocky ridge about a mile from the edge of the greenery. It wasn't much in the way of defence, other than that siege engines had to be disassembled and then rebuilt on the flat plains outside Noorinia's walls, and a loaded wagon had to slow to a crawl and be helped along, but...

The ridge extended far enough out that any siege encampment was restricted to the plains. Bandits could set up small camps of a dozen or so each in the ridge itself, but an army couldn't scatter in such a way, and camping on the other side of the ridge left them too far from Noorinia to mobilise each day.

Most armies, anyway. When Owain finally brought his forces together, their strategies would be very different to the ones Mal had faced before. Owain also intended that they would be far more successful.

Then they crested a final ridge, and Noorinia came into full view. Owain had been wrong; he wasn't ready to see his home again.

The sun gleamed where it reflected off the windows of the palace, and the springs and fountains that provided water. Here and there, trees could be seen over the walls, date-palms and myrrh and the occasional fruit tree. If Owain closed his eyes, he could almost see the streets and gardens he had once played in...

His memory provided him with images of those same streets running red with blood, houses and trees on fire until the Warlord snarled at his men to put them out, the goal was conquest, not destruction. He stumbled over a body, looking at the bloodied face and seeing his father's eyes staring blankly into oblivion... Owain blinked, and the images faded. Rather viciously, he kicked the rock he had nearly tripped over, sending it flying off into a shallow dip.

It vanished not with a clatter of stone on stone, or the soft thud that would have resulted from hitting sand, but with a metallic clang.

Instantly, Owain was on high alert, signalling to the rest of his company to be ready for an ambush. He spotted one guard, thankfully not of his company, who was clearly daydreaming and had missed the signal. Owain scowled, and opened his mouth to shout a warning, but too late.

Bandits poured out of the hollows on both sides, at least a score of them. Fortunately, the rest of Owain's forces had been paying more attention than the straggler, and were not caught off guard. "Shields!"

The shields had been Khial's idea, able to use singularly or interlocked as a defensive barrier. Owain caught the sword descending toward his face on his own blade, kicking his attacker hard in the kneecap, and decapitating him as his leg buckled beneath him, and the battle was on.

Quinn and Gerin were spaced out along the supply train, holding the line when others faltered, trying to gain enough room to properly form a shield wall. Being mounted would make it a lot easier to co-ordinate the battle, but there was very limited room to manoeuvre, making ground combat far more realistic. Owain threw a dagger, killing a bandit who was trying to sneak up on Quinn's blind side, and dispatched his current opponent with a vicious upward swing. Another came at him with a cudgel, and Owain slid in close, deflecting it with his bracer-protected forearm and driving his sword into the bandit's heart.

The bandits had slightly greater numbers, but their tactics relied on surprise and overwhelming their opponents before they recovered. Owain's forces had been prepared for their ambush, and reacted swifter than the brigands had anticipated. The battle was not a long one.

Owain glanced around, assessing the damage. There were some injuries, but none so severe that they couldn't wait to be treated. One of the wagons was missing a spoke in the back wheel, and the cover on other was torn, but the contents seemed undamaged. Owain picked out the daydreamer and two of his friends done a particularly shoddy job of defending themselves; if there was another ambush, he didn't want them on the front lines. "We keep moving! You three, support the wagon around the damaged wheel, and be prepared to carry it if you can't do that properly and we lose the wheel!"

The priority was to get the wagons safely to the besiegers, before any other bandit groups came to join in the fun. Bandits were like carrion-eaters; happy to go after prey that someone else had already killed, rather than doing the heavy work themselves. Owain would prefer no further delays.

Lecturing the lacklustre guards could wait until he was less preoccupied, and could shout at them properly.

*   *   *

The Quartermaster had been grateful enough at the timely arrival of supplies that he loaned Owain the use of his tent while he oversaw distribution and storage.

When he returned the other guards to their own company, the majority of whom were recuperating from a bloody campaign in their guildhall, Owain would have to suggest that their swordmaster remind them of the basic principles of disguise. As in, *not* standing in the line of the sun so they formed perfect silhouettes against the tent wall. That was for later, though; right now, his focus was on the dreamer who had returned to reality long enough to realise that he was in for an official reprimand of epic proportions.

Owain let the guard sweat a little, then pinned him with the kind of disappointed-angry stare that Meri was so good at. "Do you have an explanation for your actions?"

The guard squirmed where he stood. "No, sir. I didn't sleep well, not so close to Noorinia, but that doesn't excuse me."

Owain frowned, briefly distracted. "What does Noorinia have to do with it?"

The guard didn't look up. "I was witness to the massacre seven years ago. I couldn't stay after that. I held out for two years, then left. Being here brought it all back, and what Lord Mal threatened to do if I told anyone that it wasn't a sickness pandemic that wiped out the previous occupants."

The guard was old enough to have been an adult during the massacre, or a young soldier. The latter was more likely, and that could be useful. Owain sighed. "In future, tell the officer in charge of your Battle Shock and the triggers. We could have considered you unwell and adapted for your absence until we were on our way back. Do not put your comrades at risk by hiding your injury in such a way again."

Perhaps he was letting the guard off lightly, but Owain was not a stranger to trauma; his own or that of others. He would ensure that the guard's captain was made aware, but take it no further. The guard practically melted with relief. "Thank you, sir."

His gratitude was more than understandable; No mercenary wanted to be named as the reason another company would not work with his own. Owain waved a hand, "Tell your comrades outside that you are not in extreme trouble and they can stop eavesdropping. Then sit down and pour yourself a drink."

Owain might have punished the guard further, to set an example, but in this case, he had another use for the man. Something far more important than setting an example. He waited until the guard had taken a seat, estimating that they still had at least an hour before the Quartermaster demanded his tent back. "Now, tell me about Lord Mal..."

Chapter Seven

Three months after Owain's journey to Noorinia, and safe return, he returned to the Desert Stronghold, for the first of what he intended to become annual meetings between the Captains.

Siria was the next to arrive, looking very pleased with herself and full of success stories. Apparently, Owain's fears had been unfounded, and the all-female company was quickly gaining a reputation as a force to be feared. Gerin and Quinn were close behind her, their numbers having grown enough for Gerin to have become Captain of a second company working closely under Quinn's, until he felt ready to strike out on his own.

Meri was the last to arrive, Lyssi in tow. It was hard for Owain to believe how much his daughter had grown, but at least she had steadied from the hummingbird-like energy of her toddler years. He plucked his daughter out of the air with the ease of long practice, and smiled at Meri, "Khial didn't come with you?"

Meri shook her head. "No, there were things that needed seeing to. I'll tell you later."

Owain could respect that, and put his curiosity aside for later. An exasperated glare convinced Quinn to stop teasing Siria before she did him an injury, and all of them settled around the table. No one really liked giving reports, but it was better to get them over with and then move on to more interesting things.

Re-taking Noorinia was still a long way off, but sharing what information he had gained from the soldier, and laying the beginnings of a plan should be done as soon as possible. The more time they had to prepare, the better.

* * *

Later, he perched on the highest crag with Meri, Lyssi curled up and dozing in his lap. She was too big now - when had that happened? - to use his crossed legs as a mini-nest, but she leaned against his chest, small face partially concealed by the tumble of red-gold curls. Owain caught the soft look on Meri's face, and smiled, "So, what is this mysterious business that keeps Khial away from you?"

It was meant to be a joke, but Meri's face grew serious. "Della is going through her own cycle, and she wants a child. Khial is the only male Avian she's not related to, and most of the other men there are either strangers, or still recovering from trauma."

Owain blinked, the unsaid words telling him everything. "How are you faring with that?"

Meri shook her head. "Oh, no, I don't mind! Della doesn't want a permanent arrangement, and apparently it's a common thing in the more communal flocks. I just... don't want to witness it, and Khial doesn't like showing off what he perceives as his weakness."

That didn't need much explanation either. Lacking wings, Owain hadn't needed to perform quite the display that an Avian male would. Khial's wings had been healed somewhat, but he would need time to recover after... ah, *helping* Della. It wouldn't be easy for the proud warrior, no matter how much he intellectually understood that there was no shame attached. "Perhaps it will soften Mas toward him? If Della doesn't want paternal involvement, Mas will be the one best able to empathise with him."

Meri brightened a little. "Della won't keep it a secret, but she's always been the more traditional of the two of us."

That was an understatement, for all that both sisters seemed to delight in scandalising their father as often as possible. Mas was lucky that only his daughters managed to elicit such reactions from him, though Quinn managed an annoyed glare every so often. Owain relaxed, and glanced down, seeing a small figure at the base of the rock formation. "We'd better go down before Anee comes up. You couldn't manage to leave him back at the Aerie with the others?"

Meri sighed. "Not unless we wanted him to sneak out and try to follow us. He's been watching the warriors train ever since your last visit, and copying them. I know it's not what you wanted, but you should get used to the idea now."

Owain groaned. "He's my little brother; I'd hoped to spare him this life."

Meri placed a hand on his shoulder, and Owain briefly regretted that they hadn't lasted as a couple. She understood him better than almost anyone. "You're also the only father he remembers, and he thinks that you don't have enough people looking out for your well-being. He wants to protect you."

Anee was already about a meter up, and Owain could think of far too many things that could go wrong while climbing in the dark. "Then our first lessons are going to be about assessing risk, and why giving your future captain a heart attack is a bad idea."

Meri laughed, gently waking Lyssi, and lifted Owain into her arms, gliding down to the sand on silent wings. On his own two feet again, Owain reached up and pulled his brother down before he could place all of his weight on a rock that was nowhere near as stable as it looked. "If you wanted to get my attention, there are less dangerous ways to do it."

His brother clung to him like the barnacles Owain had seen on ships the last time he escorted a merchant caravan across the desert to a trading port. "I missed you, and you've barely spent any time with me yet."

Owain tried not to feel guilty; he had a lot of responsibilities, and they wouldn't be shrinking in number anytime soon, but he should have made more of an effort for Anee. On the other hand, acting out to get his attention was not a habit Owain wanted to encourage, in Anee or anyone else. "Next time, just say so, and I'll do my best to make time for you. But being Captain is a lot of work, and I won't always be able to do so right away."

Meri led the way back to the caves, Lyssi already asleep again in her arms, the Avian woman hovering a few feet off the ground to avoid jolting their daughter. "This is why communal child rearing is better. Then you have multiple people to go to when you need help."

Anee looked confused, and Owain resisted the urge to roll his eyes. "You're being too subtle, Meri. Anee, she means that if I'm not available and it's important, you can talk to her, or Khial, or Della, or Mas, or anyone else who is available. I don't need an excuse to spend time with you."

Anee considered this, then held out his arms like Lyssi sometimes did. Owain sighed, and swung his brother onto his back, bracing his legs for the weight of an almost-ten-year-old. "You're getting too big for this, but fine."

His brother's arms draped around his neck in a hug, and suddenly nothing seemed as dire as it had an hour ago. Owain ignored Meri's knowing smile, and decided to enjoy the next few days before they parted again.

Chapter Eight

By the time two more years as Mercenaries had passed, Gerin was a captain in his own right, his smaller company rapidly growing. Brek had likewise become the head of their sixth company, largely comprised of former slave-gladiators, most of whom were of races adapted to survive the harsher desert.

That, at least, gave Owain someone other than Mas able to keep watch over the deeper desert, guarding the freedom trails and working with Meri to intercept the Slavers who had figured out that the main roads were no longer as safe for those who traded in lives as they had been.

Descendants of the Lizard-Men made for popular gladiators, apparently, able to withstand even the worst of the mid-day heat that sapped energy from everyone else, which meant exciting fights, rather than gladiators staggering after each other in a slow chase until one of them collapsed. Perhaps that resistance had to do with the smooth, hairless skin that on closer inspection was covered with tiny scales, the biology that was neither as properly cold-blooded as their reptilian ancestors, nor quite as warm-blooded as humans. Either way, they were formidable in a fight, their long, forked tongues enhancing their already keen senses.

Close behind them in popularity were the Pantera and the women of the Leonine folk, akin to the great cats from whom their names stemmed. Fierce and deadly, their bodies were covered with a fine layer of hair, with the exception of their human head, hands and feet, fingers and toes ending in claw-like nails. The Pantera shared a similar hairstyle to Mas's flock, a multitude of long braids, while the Leonine preferred to allow theirs to flow free, held back by elaborate head-pieces that doubled as helmets. Like Brek, they were fast enough on two legs, and capable of astonishing bursts of speed when they dropped to all fours.

Many of the Leonine joined Siria or Meri's forces, more used to working with other women than in mixed groups. Some of the Pantera women joined them, while others remained with the menfolk in Brek's company, led by his second, Reen, one of the rare Leonine male warriors.

Now, almost six years after their first venture as Mercenaries, they were in high demand, and cautious inquiries were being made.

A heavily scarred man who moved in a way that marked him as a veteran of many battles, doing a very bad job of acting casual - honestly, he made the newly teenaged Anee look subtle! - put Owain on his guard in an instant. "Can I help you?"

The veteran looked displeased at being caught out, but rallied quickly. "I hear that there are some newcomers on the mercenary scene. I need someone to guard a slave convoy-"

Owain cut him off, not waiting to hear the rest. "My company doesn't deal in live cargo."

The veteran nodded. "That's what the others said, too. I suppose you're old friends. They [Who?] would hear nothing more from me, though I have a much more lucrative offer."

Ah, so he was on an intelligence gathering mission, as well as recruitment. Well, their refusal to work with slavers was common knowledge, and Owain had missed playing the game of leading people in circles while giving them the impression that he was telling them everything. "We trained together as company leaders, I suppose a few things were bound to rub off."

The man's hand touched an amulet, recognisable as one that alerted the wearer to a lie. How fortunate that every work Owain had spoken was true, if an incomplete truth. The veteran tried again, "I represent a powerful man in need of help to defend his lands. He has an army, but many of them are no longer young men, and the youth of our city are not yet old enough to replace them."

Suspicion tugged at the back of Owain's mind, and the sight of another mercenary Captain, Oneka, who he had teamed up with a few times in the past, heading their way with a scowl did nothing to dispel it. "So your master needs help to break a siege, I take it. Where? I can't and won't commit to something if I don't know the details."

The man scowled, clearly having wished for a promise from an eager youth before he filled in the blanks. That, in itself, was a large red flag. "Noorinia. He-"

That explained why the man was having so much trouble. The Butcher of the Desert did not have a reputation that encouraged anyone to willingly put themselves under his power, and Companies that accepted gold in exchange for committing atrocities were quickly shunned. Mercenaries fought for gold, but they valued their honour and reputation more. Owain cut the man off before he could press further. "Lord Mal does not have a good reputation. If I accepted your offer, I would lose the trust and respect of every other company, and none of them would work with me again."

Captain Oneka, stopping just out of the man's line of vision, relaxed. The man didn't, scowling fiercely. "My Lord cannot promise a permanent arrangement at the present time, but perhaps a retainment..."

In a few years, when it came time to plant his own people in Noorinia, that would be an ideal option for a small squad. Perhaps it would be better to avoid isolating the man entirely. Owain made a habit of keeping one eye on the future, after all.

Feigning disappointment and making a tiny gesture that only Captain Oneka could see, Owain shook his head. "I regret to say that my Company has been committed elsewhere for the time being. I will keep the offer in mind, however."

The veteran scowled, but accepted his answer without aggression. Owain was mildly impressed; the majority of Lord Mal's men that he had come across (and subsequently killed) rarely showed such restraint. He waited until the man left, then gestured for Oneka to come out from where he had been lurking in the shadows of a market stall. "Has he approached everyone yet?"

Oneka was a tall man with the smile and opportunistic tendencies of a travelling salesman, but if he called you friend then a more loyal ally was hard to find. He leaned against a stall, offering Owain a drink from a belt-flask. Owain accepted and sipped it, knowing from experience that it would not be water. Oneka pouted slightly when Owain didn't choke on the strong liquid, and returned to business. "Very nearly. His offer is high enough that I've had my men warning the less experienced captains to get details first. No need for them to ruin their prospects for a mistake."

That was why Owain stayed cautious friends with the other Captain. Too many would leave newcomers to flail and sink, in the interest of avoiding future competition. Oneka would steer them away from serious mistakes, but still let them learn on their feet. It was probably why no-one had killed him out of sheer aggravation, yet.

Captain Oneka looked at him seriously, "I thought you had enough sense not to need the warning, young one. Why did you not refuse?"

Owain ran a hand through his hair. "I don't have a lot of foresight, but there will come a day when I need someone inside Noorinia. Rejecting him outright... long-term, it would have unfortunate consequences."

That was a distraction, more than anything, Oneka's eyes gleaming with opportunistic delight at the idea that he had a contact with even a hint of the Seer's Gift. (Owain had taken pains to keep Oneka and Quinn away from each other) It worked, though, and the two Mercenary Captains parted ways. Owain returned to his company with a spring in his step. Slowly, but surely, his plans were coming together.

Chapter Nine

Meri drew the sobbing, newly-freed slaves into the fold of her people, who would deliver them to Della's care. Lyssi had joined her aunt in that duty, at least while her new cousin, Calen, was young enough to need near-constant attention. Mas hadn't been thrilled that his grandson favoured Khial, with wings of pale lavender and tanned skin much closer to his father's shade than Della's, but it didn't stop the older Avian from adoring his grandchildren as much as he did their mothers.

Owain stood with Siria, a squad of her Company standing guard over the prisoners. Behind them, a brothel burned, and a finely-dressed man alternated between glaring at it, and at Owain. Those who had run the slave-stocked House on his behalf had heard the rumours of the mercenary companies who targeted the slave trade, and were sensible enough to keep their eyes down, apprehension at their immediate fate radiating from their hunched postures. They were right to fear. Siria was not known for mercy to those who trafficked in people, and Banti, now acting as her second and Company Healer, was even less so.

The finely-dressed man, the elusive owner of dozens of slave brothels and with a close connection to Lord Mal, one of the few who frequently travelled outside Noorinia and who they had been trying to find for years, had no such wisdom or self-preservation.

Owain touched Siria lightly on the shoulder. "See what information you can get from them, first. We don't want someone unknown to simply step into his place."

Siria glanced at Meri, and they exchanged nods, before Meri went to speak briefly with the newly rescued slaves. Siria turned to her own forces. "Take them back to our camp, that way they can't call on the city for help."

She turned back to her old friend, "Owain, can you go and make sure that the city officials know that it isn't in their best interest to get involved in a private bounty contract? It would set a bad precedent."

Owain raised an eyebrow, "You finally got someone willing to commission you for these missions?"

Slavery was profitable, too profitable for many people to offer any contract more involved than retrieving a lost relative. Someone offering a contract of this size was either paying a pittance, paying a lot of money to get the bounty hunter to walk into a trap, or trying to get a leg up on the competition. Either way, it was an occurrence worthy of note. Siria nodded, a vicious grin betraying her serious mien. "Lyssi offered us a gold coin and a batch of honey cakes. Technically, it counts."

Perhaps not so nefarious, then. Owain made a mental note to talk to his daughter about this when he saw her next. If nothing else, to ensure that she knew this kind of bounty payment was the exception, not the rule. Siria laughed at his expression. "She wants to contribute, but knows that she's too young to be permitted to join us. It was clever, to find a way around that."

Too clever, really. As if Anee wasn't trouble enough in terms of precocious children that Owain was somehow supposed to raise!

Meri returned, her eyes sparkling at whatever expression he was making. She started to undo her leg-wrappings, revealing the lethal, raptor-like claws that she usually hid, "I've got a rough idea of the hierarchy. Find somewhere else to be for the next few hours. We'll bring you a report of what we find out."

Part of Owain wanted to protest that it wasn't fair of him to ask them to obtain answers in ways that he didn't. Another part knew that Siria needed the reputation boost, because despite all evidence some people persisted in thinking that 'female' meant 'gentle', and that as the most prominent of the Mercenary Captains, his reputation needed to remain clear. Reluctantly, he nodded and turned away, ignoring the suddenly-pale faces and cries for help or mercy as Meri's talons, and a multitude of Pantera and Leonine teeth and claws were revealed.

He had almost reached the administration district when the faint, distant screaming started.

*   *   *

Owain's experience of Avian flight had been an enjoyable one, and Meri had been careful with him.

From the number of dislocated or broken limbs, most of them with bleeding talon or claw wounds, the interrogated prisoners had not been so fortunate. Siria was looking as though she'd found hidden treasure, as were the Company Scribes busy compiling everything into a formal report. Meri was pre-occupied with cleaning and re-wrapping her feet, the awkward hopping dance as she tried to avoid scorched feet a stark contrast to the lethal grace Owain was more familiar with.

Nera, one of Siria's Leonine warriors who had been willing to share her name with an outsider, was cleaning her hands and claws, tail lashing in excitement. "You'll like what we got, Owain. Gerin is going to like it even more."

Gerin and Nera had some kind of relationship best described as friends with benefits and occasional emotional sharing. Owain made a point of staying firmly out of his friend's relationships. This, however, was not the sort of thing Nera would normally insist Gerin would enjoy. "How so?"

Nera gestured to the lord. "Among other things, he's the one who enslaved Banti and killed their older sister. Gerin's been looking for him for a long time."

Gerin *would* be pleased... and then worried and depressed at the darkness it brought out in him.

Owain made a mental note to abuse his power by taking himself off the clean-up detail. Someone else could deal with the aftermath of his heart-brother's sure-to-be-messy vengeance. "Well then, he certainly isn't leaving this place alive. I think Banti gets first dibs, though."

Banti looked up from where she was helping Meri's healer to tend assorted injuries. "Tempting, but no. Vengeance is... dangerous for a Healer. I'll be satisfied knowing that he's dead. Meri, are any of yours in a mental and emotional state where they'd benefit from being able to deliver justice to their abusers?"

Meri's smile was distinctly remincent of a hawk who had just spotted a rabbit. "I'll go find out."

*   *   *

Gerin wasn't pleased that Mal's second was nearly dead before he got the chance to have a go at him, instead of merely finishing the job, but was at least satisfied with his confirmed death as he sat down with Quinn and Owain to go through the results of the interrogation.

Quinn let out a low whistle. "Well. this is why we bother to ask questions before we kill people. Do you think Mal was even aware of how much this man knew?"

Owain had thought the same thing, which is why he had called for back-up in reading through it. "In terms of blackmail, probably. That he was quite this aware of Mal's forces and plans... almost certainly not."

Gerin tapped the paper he had been reading. "I admit, I didn't expect to find out that the bastard had more than one child. An heir is one thing, but two bastards as well?"

Quinn shrugged, "One of whom called that snake we just killed her father. Maybe the Butcher was trying for a son, or maybe he just didn't bother with precautions. He seems the type."

Owain wished that two of his best strategic minds were less easily distracted. "Either way, it's useful information to know. Evacuating the Heiress along with the rest of the interlopers wouldn't have ended well for us."

Gerin winked at his oldest friend. "At least they're old enough that I won't feel like a creep seducing one into opening a gate for a midnight meeting."

Owain tried not to sigh; he'd thought the same thing. The easiest way to get into somewhere was to have an invitation, and the best way to get an invitation was usually through seduction. "Worry about that when we get to Noorinia. For now, we need to get copies to our trusted Captains so they can review it before the next summit."

Quinn leaned back in his chair and hastily straightened again after nearly toppling over. "That's the good thing about having a genuinely evil enemy; nine times out of ten, everyone hates them too much to bother betraying you."

Had Owain's father had to deal with this kind of nonsense from his Advisors and Captains? Nothing could make Owain give up on finally returning home, but there were definitely times that he regretted being the Heir to Noorinia's throne. Leadership, and eventually ruling, was far more complicated and less enjoyable than the Bards made it sound.

Chapter Ten

The information gleaned from Mal's second had proven akin to a goldmine.

It hadn't gone to waste. Owain's people had used some of it to improve their long-term plans, and the rest to make life difficult for Noorinia's invaders in a dozen little ways.

 Delayed or lost supplies, not essential, but little luxuries Mal's people were accustomed to. Waylaid messengers, so that bad news always reached Mal first, and the warlord's perpetual bad mood trickled down to everyone else. Inconveniences, nothing so severe as to provoke action or retaliation, but enough to be noticeable.

Noorinia was one of the few places in the region where Slavers could go without fear (Owain had so many opinions on his home getting such a reputation, even if everyone knew it was only because of the current Lord.) Siria and Meri stepped up their efforts in that direction, and a letter from Oneka suggested that Mal's recruiters had stepped up their efforts from warriors-for-hire to anyone young and fit enough to hold a sword. With each new report, the feeling that something was coming to a head intensified.

It didn't feel like a warning of trouble to come, in Owain's limited foresight, merely that Change was on the wind, and that he should be on his guard.

His Captains were cheerfully laying plans for at least another hundred irritations, and Meri and Della were on the verge of creating a third company of Protectors with the number of freed slaves.

Anee, who Owain had utterly failed at keeping from the Mercenary life, was getting some much-needed experience in leadership without his older brother to lean on or back him up. Owain tried not to fret too obviously when reports reached him about yet another daring plan pulled off at the last second, and thanked whatever gods or guardian spirits might be listening that Lyssi seemed more inclined to follow in her mother's talon-prints. Of course, with the aforementioned third company looking more and more likely, and in need of a leader, that idea wasn't as reassuring as it could have been.

Bards had a lot to answer for, in Owain's opinion. Parenthood was never this stressful in the epic stories he had listened to from marketplace storytellers, before Noorinia fell.

Of course, those had been stories tailored for children, a way to pass the time under a shaded canopy on a hot afternoon. The child Owain had been was more interested in grand adventures than the details of adult responsibilities that had seemed so far away at the time. Foolish, perhaps, but Owain was glad to have those happy, carefree memories to look back upon.

His life was difficult enough that having a few good times to remember was always of value.

A flutter of wings was all the warning he got, narrowly dodging a flying tackle from a red-gold blur of exuberance that resolved into Lyssi. "You aren't supposed to dodge, Father!"

Owain hugged her, wondering when she had become so tall. Of course, little was known of Avian growth rates, other than their long life-span. Perhaps they reached maturity earlier, then their aging slowed? "Your targets won't stay still for you to catch, dearest. Why make it so easy for you?"

Lyssi pouted as stronger wingbeats heralded the arrival of an adult Avian. This time, it was Della and Mas, who flew on to break up an argument between Gerin and Quinn. Owain knew both of them well enough to know that it was boredom and dramatics, rather than true ire, that fuelled the performance, but if Mas wanted to spare him the trouble of dealing with it...

Likely Mas had come as extra protection for Della, who accepted his protectiveness more easily than her independent sister, which made

Owain wonder what could have caused Meri's absence. Perhaps it was as simple as Della wanting to introduce her new nestling. If that was the case, then Owain was honoured at the trust Della showed in bringing the vulnerable chick so far from the nesting ground.

Della landed gracefully, adjusting the sling across her chest as she kissed him on the cheek in greeting. "Calen almost made it, but fell asleep on the final stretch. Meri and Khial send their greetings."

Owain peeked into the sling, where downy lilac wings were wrapped around a small body the colour of the rare and expensive cinna bark, a spice that had required the protection of Owain's full company for a few jars. Dark blue eyes opened, regarding the young warrior sleepily, and Owain stroked a gentle finger over the dark fuzz that crowned the small head. "Mas must be thrilled at the potential of being less outnumbered than usual."

Della laughed softly, "He admitted to being incorrect in his estimation of Khial, who proclaimed it the nicest thing Father has ever said to him."

Lyssi shook her head, swinging gently off Owain's arm. "Grandfather says a lot of nice things about Papa. Just not where Papa can hear him."

That did sound like Mas, and it was good to heal Lyssi refer to her mother's husband in such familiar terms, especially since Khial was shouldering so much of the actual child-rearing when Owain and Meri had to be away on missions. Owain blithely ignored the hard stare being directed at him from where Mas was perched on the next peak over, should he have any plans of repeating Lyssi's comment to anyone else. Besides, he doubted that anyone would believe him even if he did say something. Just as Owain would never betray Khial's confidence that he enjoyed the verbal sparring with his father-in-law too much to give it up now.

Della merely looked amused as Owain swung his arm high, launching Lyssi into the air, where she promptly settled on his shoulders. "Not even of age, and she's already got both of your gift for intelligence gathering."

Owain winced, "Stop giving her ideas, I already spent most of last year dissuading her from raising her own army and paying them with Sage leaf."

While common, the herb only grew in the high mountains, making it valuable enough to use in barter. Lyssi folded her arms and wings with a huff that reminded Owain of her mother, and that Lyssi was still a young adolescent. "Mama said that I'd de-value the market."

Owain tried not to laugh, and Della shook her head. "Either way, Meri says that she'll see you soon, even if she doesn't make it to the summit.

There are some rumours that she wanted to chase up, first."

That could mean any number of things, but if Meri wasn't telling, then it was either very important, or too vague to specify. Owain shook his head and resigned himself to waiting. "Did she say anything else?"

Della shrugged. "Only that you should start putting your dreams to parchment. I didn't know that you'd taken up drawing."

For a moment, the world seemed to stop around him. Of all those close to him, Meri had the best information network of his Captains. She was also the one he had spoken to most about his dreams of finally returning home. If she had missed this year's meeting for the sake of investigating a rumour...

Well, the meeting itself would take up enough of his attention, and if Meri made it back in time, their makeshift council could discuss it then.

He shook his head and smiled at Della, then left to round up the rest of his Captains. If they were to start laying plans, then Owain would prefer to get the routine matters out of the way first. Besides, anything that gave his oath-brothers something to do besides needle and bicker with each other was better implemented sooner rather than later.

*　　*　　*

The annual review took only a few hours, and Owain found himself walking the perimeter with Quinn. They were within shouting distance of the camp, but far enough away to allow a certain amount of privacy. Owain valued that, the time alone where they could just be friends, rather than Captain and Commander. "What was all that between you and Gerin, earlier?"

The Seer shrugged, muscled shoulder's rippling, "Just Gerin being protective. It's resolved."

Owain hoped that didn't mean Quinn had been flirting with Nera. His friend continued before he could ask what Quinn had done, however. "Would you like my company later tonight?"

Owain blinked, less surprised by the proposition - it wouldn't be the first time he and Quinn had been casual partners - than by the fact that the Seer had actually asked. "Normally I just find you in my bedroll and have to decide on the spot."

Quinn hummed, "Yes, apparently Gerin thinks that doing it that way shows a lack of respect for you and your authority, or something."

Owain considered the question. "I don't know if I'm in the mood for sex, but I'd never actually turn your company away."

Quinn smirked in a way that went straight to Owain's groin, and made him even more thankful that neither of them wanted to be anything more complicated than friends. "I look forward to it."

Chapter Eleven

It was on the last day of the summit that Owain looked up as a shadow passed over him, shielding his eyes and ignoring Anee's squawk of annoyance at sand in his eyes as Meri landed. "What did you find out?"

Meri brushed sand off her clothing. "The army you took supplies to wasn't the first, or the last. Noorinia has been under siege for years, and as soon as one force leaves, another moves in."

That wasn't precisely news to any of the Captains, but Meri had a habit of establishing background information before she imparted the meat of her news, in the interest of not having to repeat herself. Gerin went very still, the same desperate, cautious hope that Owain had been trying to suppress dawning on his face. "Have any succeeded?"

The Avian shook her head, "Not yet. The early days were other Warlords, but it's cooled down to people holding a grudge against Mal, and a pastime for Mercenary bands between jobs. Short-term training, as it were."

Siria leaned her chin on her fist, thoughtful and calculating. "How difficult would it be to persuade them to go away, do you think?"

Owain had accumulated a lot of favours over the years. A request to give the troops he commanded a shot at Noorinia would be far less than he was owed. "Not very. As Meri said, it's more about inconveniencing Mal than it is hoping for any real success. He didn't exactly make himself popular. What are you thinking?"

The sly, cunning smile on Siria's lips had struck terror into men with twice Owain's bravado. "I'm thinking that Noorinia is nearly impenetrable when the inhabitants are on guard, but once that guard is relaxed..."

Owain bit his lip as memory threatened to overwhelm him. Fortunately, Reen took up Siria's line of thought, drawing the group's attention, "Once the sieges end, and some time has passed, they'll have to open up their doors to trade, at least."

Owain nodded, forcing himself to focus on the present and leaving his memories in the past where they belonged. "Even before Mal took over, Noorinia couldn't sustain its inhabitants by the Oasis alone. If Mal's army brought their families over once they settled in, the population is at least as large as before, and years of siege take their toll on natural resources."

Gerin began to smile, "They'll be wary, but no merchant would think of undertaking such a trip without guards for his caravan."

Owain yanked them back on track before anyone got too carried away. "We will need scouts, and we don't know how long it will take before they open the gates. We aren't ready yet, either, and we won't get a second chance at this."

Quinn shrugged, less invested in the hypothetical, for all that he was supportive of his fellow Captains. "What have we but time, though?"

He had an annoying point. Owain inclined his heads. "Everyone keep your ears to the ground, and send at least one scouting group to assess the situation. We'll meet back here in six months."

*   *   *

At best, Owain had hoped that the besiegers would be amendable to him calling in favours to leave Noorinia alone for a while.

The reality, reported by Mas when they gathered again, was both better and worse than he had hoped. "The armies are withdrawing, and rumour says that there will not be more."

A temporary withdrawal was one thing, but permanent? That was something different entirely. "Why? Could it be a trap?"

Meri, emerging from her father's shadow, shook her head. "Unlikely. Mal's daughter and heiress has reached an age where he's looking at potential marriage alliances. Anyone with the money or might to be considered doesn't want to jeopardise that by having their army camped outside Noorinia."

Gerin raised an eyebrows at her, "And what of the rest? The ones who aren't likely to be considered, and know it."

Mas shrugged. "They have either enough self-awareness to know that they can't keep a siege going by themselves, or figured out that they prefer Noorinia as a potential stop along the trade roads than as a challenge to fail against."

This could still work in their favour, though it did restrict the timeline a little. "How long will it take between the withdrawal and Mal relaxing his guard enough to open the gates, do you think?"

Meri waved a hand, indicating the lack of a firm timeline. "Perhaps a year? He'll guard against tricks and traps, but if we can get someone on the inside, we will be able to use that time to get some of our forces within the walls."

A lovely thought, but unlikely. Mas seemed to agree with Owain's unspoken thoughts. "You'd need to have a way over the walls for tha - Oh, no, Meri. Absolutely not!"

Owain barely noticed the near-shout, his vision edged with silver. So that was why it had seemed so important that Anee have at least some experience as a Captain. The foresight that had compelled him not to sever ties with Mal's recruiter finally fell into place.

To be fair to his old teacher, the young Commander was no happier about his vision than Mas was about Meri's implied decision. "This was not what I had in mind when I wanted him to learn discretion."

Quinn patted him on the shoulder as everyone else sent Owain confused looks. "At least that vision finally makes some bloody sense."

Brek raised an eyebrow, "If, perhaps, you would care to enlighten the rest of us?"

Owain scrubbed his hands over his face. "That recruiter of Mal's is getting desperate. All Anee needs to do is make some noise about getting out of my shadow and gaining some proper experience under someone who knows how to wage war. That'll get him inside Noorinia in a heartbeat."

Nera tilted her head, "But also closely watched. It's a good idea, but only a fool hunts with only duck arrows in their quiver."

Owain tried very hard not to think of the dangers inherent in the task he was about to request. "As much as I truly hate it, Meri and Khial are still probably the best we have at moving undercover."

His once-lover was shaking her head before he had even finished speaking. "Not Khial. He's not so recovered that he'll be able to stand in the Butcher's presence and not react."

Mas looked as though he had taken a bite of a particularly unripe fruit. "I want to be very clear that I am not supportive of this idea."

Meri wrapper her arms around him. "You don't have to be, and we'd think a bit less of you if you were. But this is necessary; and it has to be me."

Quinn carefully manuvered himself to the opposite end of the cavern to Mas, with at least three people between them. "I foresaw it a long time ago; it needs to be Meri, or we won't succeed."

Quinn was probably fortunate that Mas didn't have room to spread his wings or easily reach the seer. At least, not before Meri managed to get in his way. "I don't want my child, or

Della's, to grow up in fear of the Butcher. I can do this, and I will."

Mas expelled a deep breath, and gave his blessing. "Then may fair winds bear you home. Just don't expect me to like it, and don't think that Khial won't be worried, either."

Chapter Twelve

To his credit, Anee hadn't let his impatience show when Owain spent several hours cautioning him about what he would face in Noorinia. He'd also taken it seriously, which made Owain feel marginally better about what he was sending his baby brother into. As much as he wanted, he couldn't shelter Anee forever, and for all that his brother barely remembered the city of his birth, Anee deserved to be part of reclaiming their home, if he so wanted.

*   *   *

At the Market, Owain sent Siria, Gerin and Banti to distract Captain Oneka and keep him occupied, while he introduced Anee to Lord Mal's recruiter.

Anee was calm and professional as he described his band's skills and strength in numbers, and avoided the more obvious traps when the recruiter questioned him on the topic of personal loyalty. That was probably a good thing, upon reflection; Mal liked people he could take advantage of, and a mercenary captain as equally skilled in diplomacy and politics as in battle was likely to be considered a threat. A young and inexperienced Captain who mostly knew what he was doing but appeared naive... that was exactly what Mal was looking for.

Anee and his squad departed as quickly as the recruiter could give them the down payment and hustle them away before a more experienced Captain could intercept them and convince them otherwise. Owain sent a brief prayer to whatever higher powers might be listening that he wasn't sending another family member to die at Lord Mal's hands, and turned away. He had his own preparations to make, and outraged questions to dodge when Captain Oneka caught onto the delaying tactics.

Which had happened about five minutes ago, to judge by the flamboyant figure that appeared in the square, storming toward him.

Sighing to himself, Owain braced himself for an interrogation, already planning a technical truth to mislead the other Captain. Oneka didn't actually know Anee, or their relationship, and Owain's brother had called in a favour recently, just not about this. He hoped it didn't take too long, Owain has his own preparations to make.

*   *   *

The sun had set on Lyssi's fifteenth birthday, and Owain sat with his daughter, watching the skies.

For this milestone, they had returned to the desert where she had been born, Siria's company having returned to the nesting ground to stand guard over those who dwelled there, freeing Della of the need for her presence, and allowing her to participate in the ritual. She and Mas circled high overhead, dark skin and wings blending in against the night sky, easier to spot by the temporary shadow against the stars than by looking for them directly. Khial paced nearby, wings flaring slightly every time he turned. Calen was at least easy to keep track of, flashes of lavender visible as he flittered between the rock spires. Owain didn't remember Lyssi having that much energy at the same age, though he considered himself at least a little biased in the matter.

Owain couldn't help but think back to a similar night, when his daughter had first hatched and he held the squalling bundle of sunrise down and wispy red-gold hair for the first time. He'd had a vision of the future that night, and looking at Lyssi now, she was the image of the young woman he had seen. Was it normal, to look at your child on the cusp of adulthood, and wish for days long past?

Owain jumped as Lyssi pointed to the horizon, "Look, there!"

Approaching from the darkness came a familiar figure, the bright emerald of her wings visible before the rest of her. Owain saw Khial visibly relax, tension draining from his own body. Knowing that Meri was able to take care of herself hadn't stopped him from worrying about his friend, alone in Noorinia, risking discovery every moment and far from back-up.

Lyssi joined her aunt and grandfather, flying to meet her mother. Owain and Khial exchanged glances, waiting on the ground; Khial's wings might have mostly healed, but he would never fly as far or as fast as he should. Better for him to wait on solid ground with Owain.

Meri was nearly unrecognisable when she landed, allowing Owain to hug her tightly, the powder in her hair and lines of dye that looked like wrinkles on her face and hands aging her prematurely. With her wings bound under her clothing giving the impression of a hunch, she would look every bit an old lady, beneath notice.

Mas landed with the desert antelope Lyssi had slain earlier, on her first solo hunt, and started to build a fire, pointedly ignoring Meri and Khial's greeting of each other. Owain didn't entirely blame him; there was only so long you could watch a couple kiss before it became awkward. Lyssi attached herself to her mother's side, and Meri wrapped an arm around her, Khial holding her other hand. "I'm sorry I missed your first hunt. How have you been?"

Lyssi could talk for hours, something that Owain ruefully admitted was probably his fault, and launched into a detailed account of her hunt.

That lasted until the antelope was cooked, and they were seated around the embers of the fire. Lyssi was dozing between her parents, and Meri stroked her hair gently. Owain kept his voice low. "What news?"

Meri didn't falter in her smooth rhythm, but her eyes were bright with anticipation, and a darker, carefully banked, fury. "Mal and his concubine deserve everything you plan to do to them, and more besides. The current besiegers are making preparations to withdraw; they'll be gone within days. If you intend to strike, now is the time to set that in motion."

Owain had waited so long to hear those words, far longer even than the time he had held any hope that it might even be an eventual possibility.

Doing some quick mental calculations, he pulled out the messenger orb that was linked to the ones his Captains carried. Quinn (acting as Owain's temporary replacement while he participated in Lyssi's coming of age) and Anee (his company having been safely ensconced in Noorinia for almost a full seven moons by now) would just be waking up. Gerin, Siria and Brek's companies were in locations where it was currently night, or early morning; Owain could contact them at a more reasonable hour.

The message contained a mere five words, but they held more meaning than an entire scroll: "It's time to return Home".

Finally, after almost half of his life spent in exile, Owain could dare to imagine that returning home - not as a guard escorting a caravan, but permanently - was actually possible.

Epilogue

Anee's squad had accepted Lord Mal's offer of employment just before the withdrawals began. With so many of his original warriors growing old, Mal hadn't encouraged him to depart when the armies and Companies that had been laying siege finally withdrew, a month after Anee's arrival. They had been inside Noorinia for nine months, now.

Meri had been in place for a year, funnelling her people into vital positions, both in the great house and in the city itself. She occasionally reported to the companies that had cleared out the bandit camps hidden in the range, and set up bases in their place, ready and waiting. Owain had seen her only once, albeit from a distance, and if not for the fact that she wore one of the matching necklaces that Khial had made as a symbol of their marriage, he never would have recognised her.

Many of those who had been freed by Owain's forces, or who had been under Della's protection and eventually left, had taken up the trade of Merchant, forming part of the giant information network vital to the Freedom Trail. Owain and Gerin's companies had split up among them, acting as guards. Reen, Quinn and Siria had divided their companies among the former bandit camps, while Brek held his in reserve at the rock formation that had been the refugees' home when Noorinia fell, where they had laid the foundations of their ambition to reclaim it.

After so many years of planning and preparing and waiting, everything was in place. They were ready for the last obstacle that lay before them.

For the second time in his life, Owain led his people through the desert toward a distant hope, and finally a home.

THE END

Sneak Peek

It had been two months since the siege ended.

Two months without the background noise of war engines and distant shouting. One month since the last of the triage shelters that treated the battle wounded closed for lack of need. Three days since Noorinia's gates had opened for the first time in easy memory.

For Sera, who didn't remember a time when the oasis city she called home hadn't been under siege by one army or another, it was strange, how much life had changed. The Lord had been cautious, wary of an army trying to enter the city by stealth, but finally, the gates had been opened and trade was starting up again. Was it truly 'again' when many had no living memory of the last time traders had passed freely to Noorinia?

Well, no matter, for they were now. Foods she had never tasted were being imported, along with cloth and spices and luxury goods that few people owned or remembered seeing. There were even people of different races, when for so long Noorinia had been populated purely by those who could pass as human, most of them retired soldiers who had been in Lord Mal's service.

Sera had seen an Avian youth, though it was hard to judge ages or indeed gender from such a distance, soar overhead, and one of the Pantera-folk could be seen relaxing in one of the many sun-soaked courtyards. A man who looked descended from the Lizard-men who dwelled in the inhospitable Hammer of the Sun, the heart of the desert where no human could survive, shouted wares from a nearby stall, the light reflecting off his scaled skin. A pair of dancing girls, like night and day, balanced swords on their heads, to the loud approval of a cluster of admirers.

It was like a glimpse of heaven, a perfect world materialising for mortals to see a glimpse of what was possible.

Sera had been brought to Noorinia as a very young child, too young to remember any other life. It was less a city than a small palace, the green oasis cultivated into orchards and gardens that sustained the Great House and the ring of houses, marketplace and wall of barracks that surrounded the oasis, protecting it. It was presided over by Lord Mal, and Sera had been companion and then handmaiden to his daughter, Persa, for most of her life. Orphaned young and with no named father, Sera often wondered if there was some kind of family connection between them, that she should share such a resemblance to Persa.

Well, it was useful. Should an invasion ever be successful, Sera could take her Lady's place, with no-one the wiser. It was a heavy burden, but Persa was kind and benevolent to her people, a far cry from her father. If a handmaiden's death was the price for Persa to replace her father's rule with something better, then Sera would pay it gladly.

But such bleak and morbid thoughts were not fit company for today.

Today, the Marketplace was full and bustling, in a way it had not been in years, and Persa had brought her handmaidens for an afternoon outside the confines of the Great House. Lord Mal wasn't so relaxed that his daughter could roam without guards, but they at least kept their distance, and the handmaidens could roam freely. Of course, today's guard were the squad of mercenaries who had arrived a year ago, and whose Captain was not as subtle as he thought about being sweet on Persa. The Lady herself did a somewhat better job of hiding the fact that she returned the sentiment.

Sera had nearly completed her first circuit of the stalls, deciding what she most wanted to purchase, when a voice came from nearby. "Excuse me."

The voice was soft, with a faint accent, and when Sera turned to look, she was briefly struck speechless. He was dressed simply, like a guard for a merchant caravan, but even the plainest clothing would fail to completely hide his good looks. Red-gold hair caught the sunlight. A neatly-trimmed beard suggested that he was some years older than her, but the face behind it was still youthful. Flowing tunics failed to hide a lean, athletic body, and his warm blue-green eyes sparkled with good humour.

Oh. Oh my.

Belatedly, Sera realised he was talking to her, and hoped that he hadn't noticed her speechless daze. "Yes?"

His smile was even more breathtaking than the rest of him. "My name is Owain. I came with the caravans, and seem to find myself lost. Could I trouble you to show me around?"

For an afternoon in his company, Sera could be troubled for far more than a walk. "I'm Sera, and gladly. Where would you like to go?"

He smiled again, taking her hand and tucking it into the crook of his arm. "Anywhere you care to show me. I promised to meet my brother by the Market Fountain later, though."

Sera had the afternoon free, and shopping could wait as long as it needed to. Persa had asked her handmaidens to check in She smiled, attempting to be as effortlessly charming as Persa. "Then come with me."

She didn't question how he had no problem turning at certain places. He had to have found his way to the marketplace somehow.

By the time an hour had passed, Sera had formed at least a dozen excuses to see the handsome man again. By the second hour, those excuses had solidified into tentative plans. She didn't resist as Owain gently steered them back toward the marketplace, but her face fell as she realised that he hadn't yet expressed interest in seeing her again.

Owain stopped, steering her into a quiet alley. "Is something wrong?"

Sera attempted to smile. "I just realised that I'm going to have to say goodbye, and I don't want to."

Impossibly blue eyes sparkled with humour. "I don't know about the Lord's immigration policies, but I'll be here as long as the merchant I'm contracted with is, and that promises to be some weeks, at least. If I haven't bored you with my company yet..."

He trailed off, and Sera could have danced for delight. "Of course! I mean, I would like to see you when we can both spare the time."

Owain touched her chin, tilting her face up as he leaned down to place a gentle kiss on her lips. "It's a promise, then."

It was her first kiss, and everything she could have wanted. The urge to throw herself into Owain's arms was almost overwhelming, but Sera managed to resist. Instead, she smiled and took his offered arm, walking toward the market and the fountain.

Persa was waiting with her guard when they reached the fountain. Most of the handmaidens were there, too, though Sera spotted the last of them, Eirna, hurrying back while straightening her rumpled clothing. Sera would get that story out of her friend later.

Strolling casually toward them, Owain whistled a few short notes, paused, then repeated them. Persa's guard whirled around as if stung, his face lighting up. Quickly, he gestured for one of his men to take his place, "Owain!"

Sera's companion laughed, gripping the guard's arm in a warrior's clasp, then pulled him into a hug. "It's good to see you in one piece, Anee."

Lord Mal didn't encourage familiarity with the guards or servants, and Sera realised that this was the first time she had heard the bodyguard addressed by name. Persa cleared her throat, and Sera hurried to take her usual place next to her. Anee looked slightly abashed. "My apologies. Lady Persa, this is my older brother, Owain. Owain, this is Lord Mal's daughter and heiress, Persa. I've been charged as her guard."

Well, good looks certainly ran in the family. Persa smiled and inclined her head. "Anee has spoken of you often. I hate to cut the reunion short, but we're expected back soon."

Owain clapped his brother on the shoulder. "By all means. Anee, we're camped outside the walls, with the caravans, if you or any of your company want to visit."

Anee nodded, "I'll work out a rotation of some kind, and see you at some point later today."

Owain bowed to Persa, ever so slightly, tossed a smile and a backward glance at Sera, and vanished back into the crowds.

About the Author

Natasja has been writing since a very young age, though those notebooks have been lost in the Old Schoolbooks Cupboard and (hopefully) will never see the light of day.

Most of her stories, published or otherwise, began life as conversations with friends that sparked an idea that grew into a story or poem.

Her publishing adventures started with poems and short stories in focus newsletters like ABA and AMBA, and online sites like Readwave, NaNoWriMo and Archive Of Our Own, before finally taking a chance with self-publishing.

Natasja Rose lives and works in Sydney, Australia, but travels whenever she can.

Her greatest wish is to visit all the places in the world that inspired her writing as a child and create new stories for new inspirations

By the Same Author

THE HIGHWAYMAN'S LEGACY

Being a Psychic sucks.

It would probably be worse if Tina Barnes had to listen to every random thought that crossed people's mind, but witnessing the death of every person who died in a spectacularly gory fashion is no picnic, either. Being on a tour of Historically Significant (read: haunted) locations isn't really helping.

Oh, and did she mention the supernatural soap opera of two ghosts possessing random people in their bid for a Happily Ever After that usually ends with the hosts dying?

Because that's happening, too.

In a chilling tale of ghostly romance, friendship and fed-up psychics, what was meant to be a normal holiday tour takes a potentially deadly turn into a race against time.

Book One of Ghostly Travels

Available in Kindle ebook and Paperback

Eternity's Invitation

Dealing with her best friend being possessed by the ghost of a star-crossed lover was just the beginning.

Returning to a place where she swore she would never set foot again, Tina Barnes is once again dragged kicking and screaming into the realm of the Supernatural.

At least she has company this time.

In the gripping sequel to 'The Highwayman's Legacy', re-join the usual suspects in a series of ghostly murders that have nothing to do with star-crossed lovers....

And everything to do with destroying anyone who has the potential to stop them.

Book Two of Ghostly Travels

Available in Kindle ebook and Paperback

All You Can Be

Living With Aspergers, by Aspies and those who love them

Asperger's Syndrome affects different people in different ways, from Aspies themselves, to people who have friends or family with the condition.

This is a collection of stories and anecdotes, ranging from the good things about being Aspie, to common coping strategies, to media misrepresentation and how it affects people of all ages and backgrounds.

Being Aspie is far from being all fun and games, but there are definitely far worse things to be.

Book One of Living Diversity

Available in Kindle ebook and Paperback

All That We Are

The Asexuality Spectrum, or Love Without Sex

We live in a very sexualised society, where sex without love is common, but love without sex seems to shock people.

In this book, we will discuss the spectrum of Asexuality, as viewed by the people who live it. This is a collection of anecdotes, ranging from discovering your sexuality, to common misconceptions and prejudice, and basic definitions of the different terms

Being diverse might come with its problems, but what's the point if you can't be yourself?

Book Two of Living Diversity

Available in Kindle ebook and Paperback

All That I Need

Childfree by Choice

Raising a family is not for everyone.

Whether because of your incompatible lifestyle, personal reasons or general disinterest in small humans, a growing number of people are choosing not to reproduce. This choice is often perceived as incomprehensible to the general, child-having, populace.

Contained within the book are a series of anecdotes from people who have chosen, for one reason or another, not to become parents. Hopefully, it will increase understanding in the community that just because you don't agree with a choice, doesn't make it wrong or invalid.

Book Three of Living Diversity
Available in Kindle ebook and Paperback

The Lost Collection

A place for my poems, short stories and other things that didn't quite merit a book of their own.

You will find short plays for all ages, parody songs, fictional monologues for historical figures, and much more.

Read about Boudicca of the Iceni and the Nika Riots, the woes of an average schoolgirl, the best way to derail a science vs theology debate, and what happens when nursery rhymes go bad.

Whether laughing at comedy or crying over tragedy, this anthology will keep you entertained through to the end.

Book One of the Anthology Series
Available in Kindle ebook and Paperback

The Writing Prompt Collection

Short stories, plus the occasional monologue and poem, inspired by writing prompts.

Read about the night-time protectors, a different take on the gingerbread witch, which industry the Millennial Generation is killing this time, and how to REALLY say it with flowers.

A fun read that will have you laughing, crying and groaning by turns, The Writing Prompt Collection is the latest in a series of Anthologies by Natasja Rose.

Book Three of the Anthology Series
Available in Kindle Ebook and Paperback

The Deliberate Collection

Short stories and the occasional poem. Read about Surviving Zombies, Alien Invasions and Dragons. Discover the fate of Jack the Ripper, and how to really get the attention of a vengeful spirit.

Alternating between funny, serious and scary, this collection of written work will keep you engaged until the end

Book Four of the Anthology Series

Available in Kindle Ebook and Paperback

Cinderella Grows A Spine

Cinderella didn't know exactly what prompted her to break free of the cycle of abuse from her step-mother, but one thing was certain: nothing is ever accomplished by waiting for someone else to magically fix things.

After all, Cinderella was a pretty, educated young lady of high birth and good breeding, and her Step-mother didn't control the world, no matter what the woman thought.

It wasn't like she didn't have options...

In a delightful reinvention of the classic fairytale, Cinderella takes charge of her own destiny, and through the power of friendship, courage and liberal applications of common sense, finds her own Happily Ever After

Book One of Timeless Tales, Modern Morals
Available in Kindle ebook and Paperback

Snow White Learns Stranger Danger

People in Fairytales are far too trusting. But what if they weren't?

Snow White learned at a young age that not everyone has good intentions, and that being a Princess didn't mean that everyone loved her.

There were people who were kind without expecting anything in return, and there probably were old beggar-women who were happy to repay a good deed, but this one was far too insistent about being allowed into the house.

In a unique re-imagining of the Classic Fairytale, Snow White learns the value of friendship, sensible precautions, and a good cast-iron skillet.

Sequel to 'Cinderella Grows a Spine'.

Book One of Timeless Tales, Modern Morals
Available in Kindle ebook and Paperback

Red Riding Hood and the Stalker

Appearances can be deceiving, but a person's true nature is impossible to fully hide.

Ruby was getting very, very sick of having to hide out at her grandmothers because it was the only place Adrian Wolfe wouldn't follow her. Really, hadn't anyone ever told him that Stalking was not romantic, and that no means no?

A retelling of 'Little Red Riding Hood', in which Stalking because you "can't stay away" is a giant red flag, and the Big Bad Wolf isn't quite so obviously a Villain. Sequel to 'Snow White Learns Stranger Danger'.

Book Three of Timeless Tales, Modern Morals

Available in Kindle ebook and Paperback

Beautiful, Inside and Out

What do you do when your arrogance and pride leaves you alone in the world? Some people lash out, falling deeper and deeper into darkness. Others learn from the experience, and become better for it. Isabella had never realised how much she would regret driving Sophia away, but she knew that before she could change things between them, she would need to change herself.

In a journey of self-discovery, friendship and the occasional scandal, Isabella realises that true beauty is found within, and that loving someone else is no help if you can't love yourself as well.

A 'twisted fairytale' retelling of Beauty and the Beast. Side-story to "Cinderella Grows a Spine" and "Snow White Learns Stranger Danger".

Book Four of Timeless Tales, Modern Morals

Available in Kindle ebook and Paperback

BETWEEN DARKNESS AND LIGHT

It wasn't Jason's fault that his father's Ultimate Sacrifice hadn't resulted in Martyrdom, but in a Villainous reputation.

It wasn't Evanna's fault that she had been in the wrong place at the wrong time, and would up with Superpowers a la toxic waste.

It wasn't Stretch's fault that his teachers focused more on using his powers than on the ethics of doing so.

In a world where Superpowers are common, and those gifted with them a facet of everyday life, the lines between Hero and Villain are not always so easily drawn.

As though being a teenager wasn't hard enough!

Book One of "Two Sides of the Same Coin"
Available in Paperback and Kindle ebook

TO LIGHT THE WAY IN DARKNESS

The first year at the Superhero Academy ended with a lot of changes, but that doesn't mean that the Super-student's problems are over.

Discrimination is still rife in the ranks, and just because things are changing doesn't mean that the underlying problems have gone away. On top of that, there are several of the 'Old Crowd' who are angry at the reluctant Superheroes as the source of all these changes, and want nothing more than to paint them as Villains.

The younger generation will need to step up their game, and keep a constant watch, if they want to survive to graduate.

Book Two of "Two Sides of the Same Coin"
Available in Paperback and Kindle ebook

A CANDLE IN THE NIGHT

A collection of short stories based around the world and characters from the **"*Two Sides of the Same Coin*"** trilogy.

Read about Alien Invasions begun and ended in ways that will give future historians some very interesting days at the office, how Supervillains formed their on Council, and how DIY costumes aren't always the best idea.

From Villainous backstories, to relationships, these stories will entertain you in the best of ways.

Side Stories from the "Two Sides of the Same Coin" Trilogy

Available in Paperback and Kindle ebook

The Time Traveller's Seamstress

Time Travel is easy. Fitting in while surfing the time-space continuum is harder.

A big part of the Time Agency's success was due to their costuming department, a variety of men and women who made fantastic clothing... and who really wished that the Agents would pay more attention to details like what year and geographical region they were heading to, and the policy on advanced notice for anything pre-1920s. Honestly, do they think all of that hand-stitched embroider and beading is easy?

A humorous read likely to make you a lot more sympathetic to the costuming department, "The Time-Traveller's Seamstress" is an entertaining book that will keep readers engaged to the end.

Book One of Supporting the Time-Space Continuum

Available in Paperback and Kindle ebook

The Time Traveller's Accountant

The Costuming Department probably had it worse, but life wasn't all roses in Finance, either.

Whether it was sourcing ancient coins in a usable condition, only for the Agents to lose then less than a week later, or trying to convince Management to approve a payroll system from the current century (seriously, did anyone still use paycheques for wages?), it was one problem after another.

You'd think that the other departments would be more sympathetic, given what the agents subjected them to, but no...

An entertaining sequel to the Time Traveller's Seamstress, this book is a fast-paced read that will keep you going until the end.

Book Two of Supporting the Time-Space Continuum
Available in Paperback and Kindle ebook

Captive Hearts

No one was entirely sure what had started the conflict with the Grey Mountains, only that there was no end in sight.

When Danae, one of the Vale's most powerful Healers, is taken prisoner in a raid, she finds an unexpected protector: Torrin, the Mountain King's nephew. In fear for her life, Danae is determined to hate the man responsible for her capture, but his kindness and compassion make it increasingly difficult.

Torrin hadn't expected to find himself in charge of a prisoner, especially such a difficult one. He hadn't expected to find her defiance so attractive either. If only she wasn't his prisoner...

Available in Kindle Ebook and Paperback

The Queen's Blade

Sayfiya was raised an assassin, but only the men of her clan are permitted to take contracts. Desperate to prove herself worthy, she plans to kill the queen who has evaded several attempts on her life, planning to succeed where her kinsmen had failed.

Instead, Queen Alexandra offers her a new life, ripe with opportunity. Accepting the offer is a risk, one that may cost Sayfiya more than she ever suspected.

Or it may lead her to something greater than she could have dreamed…

Available for pre-order in Kindle Ebook
Due for Release September 30, 2020…

The Murder Mystery

Ramona Bates thought that a dating site that matched people based on their internet search history was the perfect way to get everyone off her back about her lack of a love-life. Ramona was a crime fiction writer, who was going to have a google history to match that?

When she met Joshua Ryan, a butcher's assistant who knew a surprising amount about murder, it seemed like destiny.

When Ramona released her first book, the local police force realised that a lot of the murder scenes matched with old crime reports. Now they are on the hunt, but will they catch the right person?

In a twisting tale that puts a new spin on both crime and romance, this book will have you holding your breath to the end.

Available in Kindle Ebook and Paperback

Surviving a Zombie Apocalypse

No-one ever thought that the Zombie Apocalyse would actually happen.

If the average person thought about a potential Zombie Invasion at all, it was to mock unrealistic movies or discuss how/if they would survive it. That turned out to be a good thing.

When the emergency call went out that the pandemic that turned its victims into something very like Zombies was not, in fact, a viral hoax, but the real thing, they had a plan.

As it turned out, the biggest danger wasn't the Zombies, but surviving the morons who though they were living a video game and had just figured out that Loot Drops didn't exist in real life…

Available in Kindle Ebook and Paperback

The Protector

All children know about the monsters. The ones under the bed, in the closet, hiding beneath the stairs... All just waiting to jump out and attack.

Children do not know of their protectors, the ones who fight the monsters, who keep the children safe, until they are no longer needed. Sometimes, that lasts a lot longer than physical childhood.

In a tale that combines that fantasy and nostalgia of childhood with the more mature outlook of adult life, The Protector is a book that will leave you longing for more.

Available now in Kindle Ebook and Paperback

Earth: The Fatal Frontier

Earth Technology was no match for the might of the Federation's Advance Research Corps.

Humans - those who survived, at least - preferred the term 'Invading Space Army', amid protests about being experimented upon. The Alien scientists found their quibbling about the ethics of non-consenting test subjects tedious, but admitted that the natives were best suited to help the research teams navigate this Deathworld.

Vera was absolutely holding a grudge over the massacre of the facility where she worked, she knew how to hide emotion and fake compliance. She wasn't a wildlife expert, but the Australian sense of humour bred a wealth of knowledge on how to inflict wildlife on unsuspecting foreigners...

The real battle for Earth's liberation wouldn't be fought between armies, but by a scattered handful of survivours fuelled by spite and a basic knowledge of how to survive a world where everything is designed to kill you.

Available now in Kindle Ebook and Paperback

Whitechapel Justice

Jack the Ripper terrorised the streets of Whitechapel, until the killings stopped as suddenly as they started.

Police were baffled; had the Ripper left the area, or been scared off? Who was he and how had he stayed ahead of the law? Why had he targeted the women? The cases remained unsolved, and History would never know more than rumour and suspicion.

Only a select few would ever know the truth. The streets of Whitechapel take care of their own…

Available now in Kindle Ebook and Paperback